MW01701441

Ivon Nova

Book Four of the
Harkentale Saga

by

Jeremy James Smith

Published by Harkentale Press

www.JeremyJamesSmith.com

Printed in the United States of America

10 9 8 7 6 5 4 3 2 1

First Edition

Acknowledgements and Dedication

Ivon Nova is dedicated to my youngest son, Tiernan, who in his early life is drawn to power. I hope you take these examples of leadership into account as you grow and your roles develop. In the words of Stan Lee, "with great power comes great responsibility." And in the words of your mother and moms everywhere, "make good choices."

Tiernan's mother, Sheena, has been an ever-greater partner to me as the years fly by, and this year she has been uniquely helpful. As we ready for our first major publicity event, she has spent countless hours on everything from editing to art to budgeting and planning. I couldn't do it without her.

And Coen, this summer has been incredible spending so much time together. From designing the storytelling experience to building our portable bookpub, I've never felt more privileged than when you spend your off-time working with me.

Of course, I need to recognize the efforts of my friend and publicist, Emily, who has kept me on-task and on-schedule with these last three books of the Cyfandric Cycle. I'm excited to see the fruits of our marketing labors!

Most of all, dear readers, I thank you for your interest and reviews. You have allowed me to write these first four books, and with your help, the Mirekkan Cycle will arrive soon, with others planned to follow. Thank you for sharing and spreading the word so that the Harkentale Saga can reach its conclusion, years hence!

Prologue

"Myriad and varied are the paths to power.

Many are born to power, a child of circumstance born into a house of note. Most of the Ivons in recent history have bled the blue blood of higher stations. But rare is the Ivon whose birth alone made them great.

Power can be and often is bought, by family, by allies, even through mysterious foreign sources that want to manipulate markets and events from behind the scenes. These often use drama to mask their true intentions, and some historical leaders raised this way have been little more than loud, obnoxious puppets, the weakest to hold the throne.

The most terrible and dangerous are leaders who work their way up the ranks, finding and taking opportunities to advance themselves in little ways at every turn. It might take years for their plans to come to fruition, but once in place, these cunning leaders can affect the Cyfandir for decades. The Ivon Prior, one-time mentor to myself and Johan C'Antrell, fell into this camp.

Then there are the rare rulers who, though often getting near power through great talent, fall into power by being in the right place at the right time, and making the right choice in that critical moment. The Ivon Nova, my compeer, classmate, and friend Johan, confronted the Ivon Prior and listed his crimes during the legendary dragon Uvrede's assault on the city.

With poetic and heroic words, he battled his predecessor in front of myself and two other witnesses of bearing and title, driving him back to his throne, where he ended the monarch's life with the ceremonial dagger that started Johan's career as an Angel.

Potentia per Sanguinem, or Power through Blood."

- From "An Ivon Rises" by Ynghild the Second

Chapter 1

Tillage

Enso and Milian, brothers in their early teens, left the farmhouse in the predawn hours, mama's hot breakfast warming their bodies. Frost sparkled on most surfaces that fall morning as they trudged to the barn where their papa loaded bales of hay onto the old wagon. Years of use left more scratches than paint, but it still served. "Good timing, boys," papa said, "the dogs made a ruckus and ran off in the night. I want you to feed the cattle and check the fence lines, starting toward the road." He pointed.

"Yes, sir," the boys said in unison, and helped load the last of the morning's portion before hitching up old Red.

Red was definitely an old horse, already being an old horse before the boys were grown enough to ride. But he liked to work, and knew when quitting time was. If he saw the sun low enough, Red was known to head right back to the barn on his own, digging a furrow if you left the plow attached.

This morning, the stalwart beast of burden hauled them along the western fence line until they spotted the cattle. They were all huddled up in one corner, as if something had spooked them. Enso dropped the hay while Milian busted the skim of ice out of the trough to encourage the cows to drink. But they all stayed clustered in the corner, cowering.

"You seeing this?" Milian asked.

"Sure am," replied the older boy. "Something's up. Help me unload so we can check the fence. I'll bet a predator forced its way in."

"Fourteen, fifteen," Milian counted. "They're all here. And I don't see any wounds."

"Bréach, I'll wager. Pack dogs. I once found a pack dead and wounded in the pasture, the cattle were having none of it. But they didn't hide after. More like they were asserting dominance. This is weird."

They finished the task in the false dawn light and got on to running the fence lines. They rumbled inside the boundary, the soft grass clipped short by grazing at the end of the warm season. They were near the opposite end of the pasture, half a mile from the house, when they saw the problem.

It wasn't Bréach. A twenty-foot section of split-rail fence was down. Not just down, obliterated. Rails and posts alike were splintered and spread like matchsticks onto the road, ruined.

"Enso, let's get back and grab rails and posts. We need to get this mended before the cattle get out!"

Enso raised a hand to his brother and dismounted. "Remember what we saw at the trough? They aren't going anywhere. But look at this."

Enso reached down where the fence had been as the sunrise illuminated the scene. The earth here looked tilled, but better turned than Red had ever managed. He dug in the loose soil to find the firm earth underneath. It was two feet down! And it went all the way across the break in the fence. Dirt and debris covered the cobblestone road beyond.

As they searched further, they saw a uniform, twenty-foot-wide swath of land had been likewise tilled in an arrow-straight line headed northwest. As they looked across their pasture, the line was unbroken. They took the wagon to follow the path of destruction until they came to their southern fence line, where the destruction continued across their neighbor's field.

The more they saw, the more they understood the cattle's dread. They turned back to the barn and ran the wagon up onto the hillock halfway there. Standing on the buckboard, they followed the line as it headed towards the rocky cliffs that bounded the mountains. Milian pointed at the cliffs, several miles off.

"Is that tree falling?" he asked his brother.

Enso looked. "Well, it is a tree, a big oak, I think. And it is moving. But I don't think it is falling."

"Wow!" Milian gasped. "It looks like it is climbing! I've never seen that before, have you?"

"Never seen it. Never even heard of it in stories. Let's go tell papa. He'll know what to do."

With that, they encouraged Red to increase his speed. He didn't hurry until Enso suggested oats might be waiting for him.

Chapter 2

A Direct Route

Indaria wrapped tendrils around her wrists as the great oak tilted back and forth. She knew that this was possible, but had never tried it before. But the capacity of the oak with its Dreamvine and sensitive cargo drove her to drive the tree to its maximum.

Vascular cambium layers flexed and bulged as they lifted large branches of roots, driving fibrous bundles into cracks in the rock face. Gray slate exploded as these bundles swelled and pulled the tree upward. Thunderous noises of tortured rock intertwined with woody creaks as the impossibly animated tree continued its ascent.

As it paused for a moment to replace roots in a higher crevice, the elf looked over her shoulder to observe what she had left behind. A line of destruction spanned fifty miles towards the port town of Canolbwynt Masnach, nearly straight. If not for the rocky cliff, it would point directly at her home forest; but she figured a several-hundred-foot rock face might dissuade adventurers from following her.

This process continued for several hours as the tree fought its way up with a wooden expression. Eventually they reached the top, clambering precipitously over a hard stone corner. Here Indaria saw things she never expected - a semicircle of stone seats, each pie-shaped section made of a different material. She considered slowing down but determined instead to come back to this place to investigate when she had a less urgent mission.

Hidden nearby, a watcher regarded this terrifying feat. She stayed hidden, but despite the obvious elf, felt a kinship with the tree and an unseen passenger. The watcher watched as the tree left the stone and started a newly tilled patch leading down the north face of the mountains.

Indaria did not notice the watcher. If she had, she would have likely ignored her, such was the importance of her cargo. It took the tree a day to navigate down the less steep mountains in front of her, racing through the foothills and arriving at the venerated pool of Sara-Thola. Here Indaria slowed the tree, bringing it to the same area that Angus had washed himself six months ago.

She guided it to an ideal spot, where it would be stable for a long time, and invited the tree to drink from the sacred water. She issued a like invitation to the vine. Both sent many runners of hungry roots into the holy elven space, drinking deeply and restoring health and vitality.

For the vine, thought Indaria, it should be more than nourishment. It should be a cleansing moment; an opportunity to reconnect with what it means to be elvish.

Chapter 3

Close Council

Aromatic steam from Johan's relaxing bath twisted up like aethereal tendrils before dissipating into the room. He had already washed, bubbles from soaps with exotic scents covering the still surface of the water. He sat, silent and still, a moistened hot towel draped over his face, pores opening.

A whispering noise with a slight, rhythmic tinkle emanated from behind him. He had been alone a moment before. Cloth rustled softly abaft[1] his recumbent head. The towel was gently removed, and Johan opened his eyes to see a blade flash across his vision.

Ynghild dipped the straight razor into the bath water to wet it. Her other hand held a frothy shaving whisk, and she skillfully applied the tight bubbles of his shaving soap to his daily stubble. She rose, striding to the strop hanging from his wardrobe; ensuring the blade was as sharp as possible.

"Good morning," offered Johan, laying perfectly still in the suds. Even his breathing did not disturb the water. This had been part of his early practices, learning to regulate each one of his bodily actions. Breathing, heartbeat, and even the energy of his thoughts were controlled and paced. "What do we have today?"

"So much," she replied, drying the blade with the canvas side of the strop. It was a ceremonial process, meditative and intentional. "Where do you wish to begin?"

"Heh. Obviously, I'd prefer to talk about the Bard Corps," he sighed, "but we should probably start with reports and intel. What are my people talking about this morning?"

---

1 Abaft, a nautical term that means astern or behind. The author decided to include the word after being introduced to it by the consummate bard, Johan.

"Vincent is starting to talk about what he sees as your lack of experience. He is sure you are going to bring the nation to its knees. We might discuss how to handle him."

"Vincent doesn't concern me. He's been jealous of me since you and I were assigned to that special project in the Academy. He's a flaccid prick."

"So, the economy then."

"Ugh. Fine."

"That is, for the most part, a positive thing." She inspected the blade, letting it catch and cast the sun. "It wasn't terrible under the Ivon Prior. Rebuilding efforts are taking up every spare worker, so our initial employment numbers are incredible. Finding workers is the hardest part right now."

"A good problem to have," Johan said, blowing a bit of shaving froth from his upper lip. The tight bubble gained altitude on the steam eddies across the bath, then dropped as soon as it was over the tile floor. "Let's send a call for our military to list their skills, and match that with rebuilding needs. We'll keep the soldiers working and build some goodwill with the same stroke."

"It shall be so," Ynghild replied, reaching for the leather half of the strop. "Would you like them to go armed as a sign of strength?"

"Absolutely not! Simple street clothes only." He tilted his head. "With a couple of ribbons pinned to their hearts in my colors. Nothing more."

"I like it." Ynghild was dressed in a deep blue toga, after the manner of Ivonian nobility. She stropped the razor to impossible sharpness, the 'shick, shick, shick' noise timed to punctuate her points. "The marina is functional but still needs significant repair. I suspect we should redirect our sailors to start there?"

"Good thinking. But let's offer them a voice. Ask what they would do to make the repaired marina better than before. Then ensure the managers vocally credit them and enact some of the changes."

Ynghild raised the blue silk scarf kept at the strop and dropped a corner over the upturned blade. The corner separated instantly and fluttered down to the floor. She stalked sensuously over to Johan's tub and knelt behind his head.

"Let's talk about the Angels," she said, intentionally flashing the reflected sun off the blade and across his eyes as she said the word, 'Angels' for emphasis.

"You know how I feel about the Angels, Yng. It is time for a new way. Less secrets. More openness."

She placed the blade at his jugular.

"Both of us got our start in the Angels. We should respect our roots. Secure the future of those who got us to where we are today." She started the shave in earnest, one slip away from taking the Ivon's throne.

"The Angels will still exist. The lightplays are a part of our city's culture, an attraction that draws people from all over the Cyfandir. But the darker parts have to end. We must build trust in our community and with our neighbors. We- hey!"

He flinched as she rustled the blade clean in the bathwater towards his legs. She giggled.

"That's a little close, don't you think?"

"Oh, I'm terribly sorry, Ivon. I want you to feel safe and secure, of course!"

"I know you better than that. And you know me better than that. My mind is made up. The Angels are going back to being what they are in the public's eye - entertainers and disseminators of information. I intend to offer them roles in the Bard Corps, to be honest."

Ynghild finished Johan's shave in silence. When she was done, his face was perfectly smooth without a drop of blood. She wiped the bowl and returned the kit to its place at the wardrobe. Johan rose and dried off.

"What of Gymdeithas Fasnach?" He wrapped the light dressing robe Ynghild offered around him and settled it over his shoulders. "Are our agreements holding?"

"They seem to be. Very little fresh news. I suspect they are rebuilding and recuperating from the battle, for the most part."

"We'll let that set a bit, then." He walked out onto the open balcony that faced south, regarding his fleet. "What of the *Queen*?"

"Alene? She's been quiet-"

"I mean my ship. The *Hidden Queen*. How long since she has come into port?"

"I'll ask, but I don't think she's been here since she was called the *Incande*."

That's a detail I never told her, thought Johan. *She really is one of the most skilled spies I've ever met.* He swept his gaze across the room to settle on her form, sitting at the writing desk making notes. *A truly amazing person. Beautiful. Smart. Eminently competent. Deadly. And yet, somehow, not the partner I desire.*

He looked east, as if toward the sun, past the marine layer that mugged the city at this hour. Towards the Veyns. Towards the partner he did want.

Chapter 4

A New Odor of Business

"I wouldn't ask anyone to do something I wouldn't do," Flannan assured his interns at the pickling vats. "And make no mistake - your work here is what keeps us in business!"

Drewdod and Bowfin exchanged quizzical looks. Drewdod spoke first.

"Do the Veynsian people pay more for things to be stinky?"

"Exactly!" responded Flannan.

"Why wouldn't they want the stone to be perfumed?" asked Bowfin.

"If it smelled good, the stone wouldn't be as valuable."

"So, the pickling process makes it stronger?" stated Drewdod.

"In a way," replied Flannan. "Some aspects are stronger."

"It's repugnant," Bowfin heaved, trying not to vomit. "I can't understand why anyone would go through this! I don't see how it makes the stone any better."

"Better is a relative term," said Flannan. "The process makes the stone more valuable."

"It might make good deodorant soap more valuable," quipped Drewdod. "It must take three baths to get this stink off!"

"Sometimes four." Flannan laughed. "I find that a good soak after work goes a long way. But it is worth it! See now, the hatch is opening so you can get the next batch going. Grab a ladle and start pickling!"

Flannan laughed as he left the younger dwarves behind to do the literal dirty work. *And I don't feel bad about it,* he thought, *I've paid my dues these past few months! If I never had to smell those pickling vats again, it'd be too soon.* The young dwarf (Flannan was ninety-two) nearly danced up the stairs with glee.

At the landing, Flannan took a moment in the sunny quay to close his eyes and let the noonday sun percolate into his skin. The warmth seemed to leach into his bones.

"I'm gonna spend a lot more time outside for a while," he said, thinking he was alone.

"You might not get too used to that idea," came a reply. It was Gierman.

They hugged, and walked into the kitchen to rummage for lunch. Gertrude was not around, so they were free with loading up plates of leftovers. Flannan's platter overflowed with cheeses, cold cuts, and sausages. Gierman concentrated on fruits, nuts, and chicken, with a healthy serving of vegetables.

"Must get tired of preserved foods aboard the *Picil*, eh?" Flannan jibed, noting Gierman's un-dwarfly luncheon loadout. "Fruits and veg don't last long in the heat, I suppose?"

"You'd be surprised. No, I'm trying to make healthier choices, that's all."

The friends ascended three flights of stairs to reach the rooftop dining plaza, which they had to themselves. Everyone else was offloading marble. They enjoyed having a moment of seniority and rank privilege.

"How is vat life? You don't smell as bad as usual."

"Gierman, it is amazing! I've finally got the interns into the swing of the process. They may not like the work, but who does? We should be able to take all the stone you can throw our way. I've even considered joining a school for swordwork to take up my spare time! And the sun is fabulous. Breathing fresh, cool air!"

"I'm really glad that duo is working out for you. Unfortunately, I doubt I'll be getting much time off over the next few years. The ship has so many nuances, and I learn a new pattern of eddies and currents on every trip to Connemara."

"Would you ever have thought to be in such a critical role outside the hearth, at our age?"

"Ha!" Gierman laughed. "No, not at all. But here we are. Life is full of surprises, I guess."

"Years, you say? You don't think you can get interns trained?"

"Years." Gierman lowered his head. "As soon as the *Picil* is ready to send off, we'll have a new ship to work. Then another. Then another. It'll take four to keep up with the demand."

"Well, being busy is a good problem to have." He wiggled his tankard, noting its emptiness. "I'm dry. Can I get you a refill? What is that, anyway?"

"Water. I'm good, thanks. Come on back with yours though. I have more to tell you."

As Flannan raced down the stairs, Gierman slid back and put his feet up. He loosened the laces on his waistband. Two yawns later, Flannan rejoined him, offering a toast.

"Here's to being busy and profitable!" They shared a quick huzzah and a short chug, then continued the conversation.

"To good investments and long partnerships!" returned Gierman. "Speaking of which, I have news about our little enterprise."

"I wouldn't call the Pickled Marble business 'little'..."

"Neither would I," agreed Gierman. "But I'm referring to *our* enterprise. Yours and mine." The dwarf allowed a pregnant pause.

"I don't recall entering into an enterprise with you, Gierman."

"I guarantee you do remember entering into this." Gierman offered a meaningful look. "OUR enterprise. Just you, just me. And now we have a new business partner on the way."

Gears ground visibly in Flannan's head. After a moment, his eyes grew wide. He looked at Gierman, looked away, and looked back again. Then at Gierman's belly. It was jiggling with laughter now.

"It's a really good thing your schedule freed up, Flannan. Like I said, I won't be able to take much time off for a few years." Gierman laughed for a long time. Flannan wasn't laughing - at least not at first.[2]

---

2 Dwarves, as discussed in previous books, are a nearly genderless society. Their language works on the premise that all are equal, with the default pronouns being masculine. All dwarves grow beards, and they tend to share a stout build that makes physical differences nearly impossible to detect. In fact, the only time they discuss gender at all is regarding parental roles, in the context of children having happened.

In this way, all remain equal. Dwarves form domestic partnerships, and sometimes offspring occur. There is no greater or lesser role. Dwarf's long lifespans give them some privilege, in that time spent parenting is relatively brief over the course of a thousand years or more. Culturally, what happens between consenting dwarves is their business and their business alone.

Chapter 5

Tour of Duty

I can't keep up this pace forever, thought Patrick. It wasn't the physical demands, of course. The blacksmith had a lucrative repair business back at the Sliver which often saw him heating, hammering, twisting, and quenching hot steel from dawn to dusk. Even now in his late forties, his physical stamina wasn't an issue. Less so with a skilled apprentice holding down the shop.

It wasn't the travel, either. Patrick had run all of these roads before, decades ago, as a soldier-turned-recruiter for the Ivon Prior. He knew each roadway, every inn, every shop, down to which taverns poured the most generously. Patrick enjoyed travel in the Cyfandir. Always had.

It was more the constant expectations. As the de facto leader of Gymdeithas Fasnach, the large man was expected to be knowledgeable on every topic from the economy to military movements to cultural and religious pitfalls. People expected him to be present at so many meetings in so many places.

And through it all, he was expected to be calm.

Cool.

Collected.

Did he train for any of this? Not directly. Elementary education in the Sliver was reasonably complete, certainly one of the better places in his nascent nation to get a start. He received some basic leadership training in the Ivonian military, where he worked his way up to a junior officer before his tour was up.

He was asked to fill in at a city council meeting almost two decades ago when mortal attrition left several surprise openings. But from there it was all on-the-job training. His staid and reasonable tone put him on the path to leading the council, and he was the leader that was ready to act when they saw the fires at Pentref.

Pentref. I'll never get those horrors out of my mind.

The actions of the men and boys of the Sliver after Pentref elevated Patrick to his current station, without a doubt. And the recent events that saw him lead the bulk of all of the people - men, women, children, and elders - to an unwinnable attack on the great city of Ivonal carved his name among others into the annals of history.

Patrick was happy to serve in all of these capacities. He felt honored to do so. But being 'on' all the time, always performing, always paying attention, always listening intently wore on him. And the incessant need to say the right thing, at the right time, in the right tone, without fail was sheer torture.

And his torture continued as he rode into the next town, repeating a familiar process. Greet the local constabulary to be announced. Find a groom to feed and tack his horse. Determine where he'd be spending the night, getting his meager gear settled, then a long dinner meeting with whatever local leaders, merchants, and social figures attended. He had just sat at the middle of a long table (he never chose the head of the table) when the whole town council poured in.

They talked about the people lost in the Battle of the North Green, and how best to memorialize them. About the plights of those left behind, and the needs that come with loss. As always, some ambitious person, barely in the fight, looking for medals and recognition. *It makes it easier that we don't have medals to offer. Thanks are enough,* Patrick thought.

For Patrick's part, he searched for the needs and talents. He suggested trades between businesses and communities. He talked about a program to get people to travel more between the different towns and villages. He even discussed a school - one for higher learning.

But the most important subject was always the coming winter. Even with the grain that was restored, the year of plenty had turned to look more like a year of tightened belts and austerity. He picked up a new idea or two at each of these meetings, and shared the best with everyone.

After the meeting and some light revelry, Patrick checked on his horse, then made his way up to the room he had rented for the night. He washed in the basin provided, and reflected as he often did. This was too much load for one man with a job. And he couldn't give up the job.

He thought of young Johnny Brightshirt, full of energy and articulate in the maximum. If only he could have corralled him into being the central leader of Gymdeithas Fasnach. But he was too slow in the asking and now young Johnny was the new Ivon - the Ivon Nova. The most powerful man in the whole of the Cyfandir.

I owe that young man a visit, thought Patrick. *I know I don't have the time, but I'll have to find it. Perhaps the next time I'm out by the Greenway. And in the meantime, I have to figure out how to keep these people from naming me 'king.'*

Chapter 6

House of the Rising Sun

The afternoon sun filtered through the ethereal curtains as they flowed like long banners in Alene's palace. Her grand table was oval-shaped, big enough to seat fifty, and her seat was at the center of the long edge at the south. It was designed to give the people seated at it a sense of uniformity, where there was no head and no lower position. The Queen's seat was only slightly higher than the others, which worked well for Alene's shorter frame.

Today, Beatrice, Gierman, and Angus sat in chairs near the Queen's, which sat empty. Alene instead sat opposite the trio, cross-legged on the table. Plates of small bites sat around them, half-eaten. In their midst lay a few dozen drawings of buildings and ships, depictions of island scenes, and different contraptions.

"...it has to be big enough," Bea was saying, "that my guests, dwarves and humans, feel comfortable. Also small enough that I can handle running the place on my own."

"Dwarves don't need much space," Angus offered. "If there is a table for eating and some sleeping alcoves, we'd be in paradise."

Gierman agreed. "It'd be nice to have a place to store some libations, of course. The lads get a bit bored after being on the water a spell."

"If I'm footing the bill," Alene said, "I'd like a room for myself. I promise to use it often! One with a sunrise window. Sunrise on Connemara is one of my very favorite sights. The best way to start the day."

They discussed warehouse space, how to keep fruit fresh in the tropical heat, and even a solar still to purify drinking water. The punch list they developed called for a large, several-story building when all was considered.

"There's not enough wood on the island to make this," Alene observed.

"Plenty of stone," Angus offered, "Give a dozen dwarves a dozen years and we'll have a permanent castle there for you. Marble, even; as it is the soundest building material there."

"A dozen years?" Beatrice laughed heartily. "How much time do you think I have left? I'm far too old to let a dozen years pass before starting this last leg of my journey. It'll have to be faster. How can we make this happen by the spring?"

"I suppose," Gierman put in, "that you could build it like a boat. Perhaps a barge. Something that would be built here and sailed to the atoll, and hauled ashore. Maybe we could commission the shipyards to build the structure?"

"No." Alene stated bluntly. "A building that size couldn't sail, it'd fall right over in a stiff wind. Capsize and sink."

"Steam." Everyone looked at Beatrice to understand. "Yes, steam. The *Picil* takes a while to get anywhere, but it isn't much sleeker than a brick, and it hauls tremendous weight. Why wouldn't we build a large version of that?"

"Still too tall," Gierman observed. "We'd need to lower the center of gravity."

And then Alene was laughing, a tittering giggle that accompanied a gleeful look on her face. She jumped up and ran off to her quarters, her footfalls graceful, powerful, and soundless.

"Does she do that often?" Angus asked Bea.

"I never know with that child," the matronly woman replied. "She is odd. And yet, I'm certain she was the right choice."

That comment swung both dwarves' heads around, more questions following. Before they could ask, the Queen ran back into the room at breakneck speed, hopping up onto the table with a little shoulder roll, then sliding to a stop in her socks right in front of the group. She was carrying a toy castle. She set the tin contraption down on the table and explained.

"I found this in a toymaker's store downtown. He said he thought it was goblin in origin, but he wasn't sure. But look what it does!"

She unfolded a small handle on one side and cranked a hidden mechanism. Music played, a dramatic, springy tune, and the battlements grew. The entire center rose steadily, crank after crank, exposing a second floor. The Queen kept cranking, exposing a third floor, and a fourth, and a fifth; each one slightly smaller than the last.

When the fifth floor was finished rising, she kept cranking, and a little flagpole popped up from the center, flying the Veynsian colors. The young queen clapped and laughed again before looking at the small assembly.

"What do you think?"

"That's a very nice toy indeed, child," Bea replied. "But it seems a bit off-topic, wouldn't you say?"

Gierman, however, was very interested, and pulled the expanded toy in for a closer look.

"Oh, this is right on subject, Bea. We might be able to do this. Can I borrow this model?"

"Of course! Just get me that sunrise window, lots of windows!"

Chapter 7

Bard Corps

In the backstage area of the Cirque du Lumieres, the Ivon Nova addressed his recalled Angels. This was the first time all three hundred were in the same space at once; indeed, a number of them had never met before.

"Welcome home, Angels." Here, in this place, Johan did not exist. Here, he was the Ivon, the head of state and the undisputed leader of this half-bard, half-spy organization. "It is good to see you all."

The company had arranged themselves in a rectangular order, with some standing against the walls, and another line seated in various poses on the floor making another level of people. Ynghild was in this line, on the opposite side of the room from Johan.

"I know," Johan started, "that this is unusual. Unprecedented. Never in all of the stories that I can find have we been called to one place. Some of you have never broken cover before. You must be wondering why I would make such a change."

Wry smiles, nods, and myriad murmurs echoed through the crowd.

"I'll share with you why I need all of you more than ever before. But first, out of all of the stories we discuss, this story does not leave the room. While it will become our story together, for now it is my story, for me to share with the world when the time is right. This is your time to choose to be a part of this story, or leave without knowing what that story is until the rest of the world learns."

He waited, and turned slowly to meet the eyes of each of the Angels, not moving on until he received at least a nod of assent. With this process, he noted only one missing Angel, Brennan. *Maybe he is dead after all.*

"For generations, the Angels have watched the Cyfandir and its peoples. We gather stories and intelligence. We sing the right songs at the right times. We tell the right stories in the right circumstances. And we've done all of this to advance the interests of the Ivon and Ivonia."

He let that marinate. It was all true. Every statement accurate. Just not… complete.

"In a world where Ivonia is the only major power, where every location save the Veyns can be reached on foot, that is enough. So what conditions would lead to it being no longer enough?"

He let considering glances and exchanged looks circulate until one woman raised a hand. The Ivon indicated that she should speak.

"It's got to do with the dragon, right? Or if we believe the dwarf's story, the dragons?"

"*If* we believe the stories?" replied the Ivon Nova. "Why would you doubt them?"

"Because it is ridiculous. First, dragons are a mere fantasy element in older, irrelevant stories. None have been seen in a thousand years or more. Then, when not one, but two pop up, the same dwarf kills both of them? Single-handedly? Unbelievable at best. Staged or arranged at worst."

"A reasonable point," the Ivon conceded. "Do any of us believe that a dragon actually attacked Ivonal? Let's see a show of hands."

Perhaps eighty percent of the room were certain that the story was true.

"I see. How many of you saw the dragon firsthand?"

That number was closer to thirty percent.

"Seeing is believing, is it not? But for those of you unconvinced, what do you think the real story is? Remember, in this space, we listen but we don't judge."

A grizzled older man, scars on his face and arms, spoke up. "Dragons aren't real. It is a story built to manipulate minds. You likely used the Lightplay to create an illusion, sacrificing parts of the city to enhance the effect."

"I can see where you might think that," replied the monarch. "But what do you say to those that saw it themselves?"

"I'd say I'm suspicious. I'd follow the money, see if they were paid off." That suggestion received some angry shouts and defensive challenges. Johan took the situation back into his control.

"All right, I hear you. Let's bring it back. Enough of us saw the attack that I think we can empirically state the existence of dragons as factual. I was part of cutting Angus Dragonbane out of the great beast. The corpse is still being dealt with outside the Eastgate.

"But here is the thing: We haven't seen dragons in so long, many of us felt they were only figments of a storyteller's imagination. And yet, here they are. Where have they been? Why did none of us know they were real? And if they are out there and coming here, what else is beyond the Cyfandir? Who else?"

At this point, the Ivon slipped into a smooth, elegant language that almost none of the Angels knew. Almost none. The grizzled veteran spoke up again, interrupting the Ivon mid-sentence.

"Foul play!" he shouted. Except that he shouted it in Elvish. And Johan understood. He stopped speaking and mentally reviewed his last few phrases, and he was pretty sure he had been speaking Elvish. Except that it wasn't possible, since he had never learned Elvish.

"...Foul play indeed," the Ivon Nova admitted. "We'll talk more later," he offered to the older man. "For those of you who aren't sure, that was Elvish. I have never learned Elvish, yet I know it now. And I've learned hundreds of stories I cannot verify, through an incident I'm not ready to share yet.

"But these new, unfathomable facts show us that the world is undoubtedly a bigger place than we knew. Nations, peoples, continents, and even dragons are out there, and they are visiting. We need to understand who they are, where they are, and what they want. And that knowledge is paramount to not only our survival, but the whole of the Cyfandir, and possibly the whole world.

"To that end, I will fund a new unit I'm calling the Bard Corps. Anyone in this room is welcome to join. The Angels will continue on, of course, but not in the same way. We'll not just be looking for the stories and situations of today, but we'll scour the peoples we can reach for their folk tales. We have an underused and mostly forgotten library here, and the archives have already been very helpful.

"So, if you wish to be a part of the Bard Corps, meet me for breakfast tomorrow in the Archives. There we will found what I think could be the most important group of our lifetimes!"

Chapter 8

Foresight, Hindsight

Thannon led the grim procession slowly, step by languishing step. They started at the doorway to the empty home his father, Bedwyn Foresight, had been born and raised in. Bedwyn's parents had passed on many years earlier, and for centuries this old home, carved into the limestone that sat upon a glass-smooth bed of grey shale, had been kept as a museum of the King and his family.

No keening in this assembly, rather songs meant to evoke memories and times beyond memory. Old songs. Songs that would have been sung in the time of Bedwyn's childhood, so long ago. The older songs were led by the elder dwarves, learned today for the first time by some of the youngsters.

They paraded by schools, workplaces, and places of note in Bedwyn's life, pausing sometimes to hear from those that knew him best. There they shared about Bedwyn's great deeds. His mistakes. And always, his renowned ability to see what would happen in the future.

Bedwyn's peers testified to the old king's secret desire to see a dragon. Not even to slay one, just to see it and to understand what real power was. This desire was reflected in some of Bedwyn's writing; he discussed the potential benefits and pitfalls of learning how dragon's fire worked, and how to make the most of that knowledge.

Eventually they sat in the grand hall, singing low and softly. Thannon walked to the dais and took his seat at his father's throne. The singers looked down, adjusting their places to stand on regular marks on the floor. After the third stanza, the room went silent. Thannon stood.

"We gather here to honor Bedwyn Foresight, our king, and my father. Let us harmonize, working together in his memory." Thannon started a low, sustained note without vibrato. Others joined in, finding different harmonizing combinations. With each new voice, the volume increased.

The harmonic drone became a symphony that might deafen a mere human. When every voice joined, the dust on the floor rose as if swept by a hundred sweepers working together in chaos. Then the body bent the pitches of their voices, a ring of dust awakening along the circular walls that rose up to form a dome above them. As the pitch rose and the ring approached the top, the sound folded back in upon itself, reaching a resonant vibration that made the dwarves' hair fly about and their beards stand straight out from their faces. They held that note for a full breath, then stopped together in an instant, silence crashing over them like a wave, drenching hair and beards to lay flat as if wetted.

Thirty seconds of a quiet so loud that heartbeats were heard from the next person, King Thannon spoke again.

"Bedwyn Foresight was one of the truly great leaders of our world and of our time. He knew how to show that while in math one plus one equals two, it is not the same with people. Demonstrations like his Harmony show that when we work together, we multiply our effects.

"Synergistic efforts pay off. And those synergies are not limited to dwarvenkind. Late in life, Bedwyn made use of goblin technology, moving troops and himself to places that needed them. When it was time, he even designed a weapon with them that he fired, in a last act of heroism, at the great dragon. While he was not successful with that kill shot, his action spared myself and a hundred dwarves of the Smaragdine by distracting and redirecting the creature.

"He recognized that times change. That norms are adjusted. That technology will advance, whether we desire it or not. Our choices are to avoid those changes, eschewing their risks and benefits, or to embrace change and find the best parts to encourage. Bedwyn, who could see the future better than anyone I've ever met, took those risks of change.

"He took those risks because he wanted the best for his people, and understood the potential synergy of helping outsiders like humans and goblins, and occasionally even elves. I intend to keep that spirit alive, seeking the best for our people and the peoples of the Cyfandir that surround us. We are better together."

The ceremony closed with the former King's people leaving bits and bobs that reminded them of their favorite personal interactions with Bedwyn at a temporary shrine. By the end, only the eyes of the portrait were still visible over the gifts and offerings. Eyes that still pierced and shone through with a deep perception and keen interest in the observer.

Chapter 9

A Leg Up

Brin, a grizzled, middle-aged man with a ruined leg and a floppy, wide-brimmed hat, hobbled into Canolbwynt, braced by a forked tree branch under his right armpit. The busy people took no note; the man was certainly not a threat to anyone who could move reasonably well. He continued through to Cam Makinesi, the goblin outpost carved into the hillside.

The residents had installed a mechanical gate, powered by a rattling steam engine. It was open here at mid-day, but Brin observed that its heavy metal elements might make a significant barrier to entry when closed. The goblin attendant looked up from his greasy bench and greeted him.

"Welcome to Cam Makinesi! What can we make for you? A rolling chair conveyance, perhaps?" The goblin eyed Brin's right side up and down.

"You are perceptive indeed," Brin replied. "I am here to see what can be done to aid in my mobility. But not, I think, a chair. And nothing that rolls. I want to be able to climb stairs and walk the trails again. And I'm willing to pay for it."

The goblin frowned, again considering Brin's plight. He shouted back into the outpost, and a young, athletic goblin came running out. They nattered for a moment in a language Brin did not know, and the youth grabbed Brin's left hand and led him inside.

Brin struggled to keep up with the goblin's typical walking pace. He saw the space open before him, a thriving, young city peopled with thousands of happy, healthy goblins. The former holt was elaborately worked sandstone lined with goblin mechanics. Pipes, tubes, and geared assemblies populated every spare space on the floors and walls.

Where side tunnels branched off, the mechanical mess formed arches, often branching themselves to head down to another machine. Brin was led into one of these passages. As they passed he could feel the heat from some of the lines. They entered a large workshop, cluttered with tools and machinery.

"This is Sergei. He is our CME - Chief Mobility Engineer. Sergei designs our steam wagons and other conveyances." The youth did not bother to introduce Brin.

"Nice to meet you, Sergei. You can call me Brin."

Sergei had not looked up from his task, which involved his whole left arm thrust, armpit deep, into a wheeled machine. After a minute passed Brin cleared his throat loudly and tried to make conversation.

"So, this is what a living goblin city looks like?" he asked.

"City? HA." replied Sergei. "This is hardly more than a primitive village. You should have seen Seljuk, the grandest goblin settlement on the Cyfandir. It was head and shoulders above this place. Still, we are grateful for a place to start anew."

"You make it sound as if something happened to Seljuk."

"You don't know? We had a disaster. Probably testing gone wrong. However it happened, there was too much damage, too much death to repair. So we came here, accepting Bedwyn's offer."

"Bedwyn?" Brin spat, "I have no love for Bedwyn. He's been too… impulsive around me lately. I don't trust him."

Sergei looked up, seeing Brin clearly for the first time, extricating his arm, one grease-soaked segment at a time, from his work.

"Just as well then. You won't have to worry about Bedwyn anymore."

"No?"

"Of course not! He died in single combat with a legendary dragon. Have you been hiding under a rock?"

"Yes."

The goblin stopped in his tracks and tilted his head, processing. Brin saw the concern in his face.

"Metaphorically. With my bad leg, I don't get out much."

The boffin regarded Brin's injury.

"I'm not a healer. Not in my vocational training. Not right for my idiom, you might say. But I have helped with workarounds, occasionally."

The goblin visibly finished collating data and nodded smartly. He walked over to a table, sweeping gears and levers off to clatter onto the floor. Reaching under the table he pulled a pin that released the tabletop from level, revealing a stack of large-format papers clamped together at the top. The goblin flipped drawing after drawing of myriad machines until he found the one he sought.

"This," he slapped a flexible pointing rod on the paper, "is the Suspended Person In Distress Enablement Rig."

"It looks like a spider," replied Brin. It did look like a spider, with a goblin sitting on a chair making up the head, and a bellows-like cover over the machinery behind forming something that looked like an arachnid's abdomen. Six jointed legs arced up from the body and over the goblin's head before coming back down to the ground. And the passenger's dangling legs completed the similarity, putting Brin in mind of mandibles.

"A spider?" The goblin engineer was incensed. "I don't see it. I see a wonder of engineering, solely inspired by seeing a need, and fixing a need."

Brin pointed at a remarkably similar-looking longlegs spider in the corner of the room.

"You can't see that?"

"Ugh, disgusting! No! And the name "spider" can't work. It is, technically, a Suspended Person In Distress Enablement Rig. Besides, spiders have eight legs. Do you want one, or not?"

Brin imagined the freedom of being able to move across the landscape quickly again. It didn't take much time to decide.

"Yes."

"Excellent," the goblin replied. "It will be expensive, of course."

"Money is no impediment."

"Good. It will take a lot more power to scale this up. You'll have to stay on an umbilical to the steam plant, of course. Perhaps a hundred-foot range? I've got a workshop in the right area of the outpost you can rent…"

"Not here. I need to be free."

"The amount of power to make a personal conveyance like this is great." Sergei considered. "Our main power plants can bleed off enough easily, but apart from a goblin workshop, it will be difficult to maintain power."

Brin thought for a moment, and knew of a place - the place - where he might start fresh.

"I found an abandoned workshop with a fantastic view, in the mountains above the old city of Seljuk. I could see spending some time there, it was beautiful."

"I won't go to Seljuk. That place is a tomb. We honor those interred there, but I will not enter."

"I respect that. But this was a goblin workshop outside the city, over it. Is that acceptable?"

Sergei considered, jotting down notes.

"I know the workshop, and what they were studying. The last crew stole the technology and left to sell it, we still don't know to whom. But yes, it would be possible there. Possible, but very, very expensive."

"As I said, money is no object. It will take me some time to reach the area; how long to build the machine?"

"Months. And I'll have to arrive to modify the workshop. There may be value in salvage at that site, as well. All right, here is the deal…"

They hashed out details in hushed tones for more than an hour, then Brin hobbled back into the city to his favorite inn. There he was able to reserve his favorite room, and after a nice dinner and some tavern entertainment, he retired. The stairs were challenging, but he made the journey.

Once he was settled in, he waited for the last lantern light to go out of the windows before feeling his way along the rafters, arriving at his cache where he had stashed money from his earlier dealings. *Such was the life of a spy*, he thought. *Was the life. As long as I can't get around, that life is over. And that makes me angry.*

Chapter 10

Folk Dance

In the dusty, underused depths of the Ivonian archives, Johan C'Antrell, the Ivon Nova, walked alone. He lit candles and lamps all around the atrium, a large open space that would usually be lit from above. The space was sixty feet tall, and vegetation or detritus fully obscured any skylights that might be far above.

When he had enough light to function, the monarch grabbed a broom and made an attempt to reduce the dust. After an hour, he had the bulk of the floor clear, if not clean. One set of large shoeprints, wider than his, had been the only disturbance in this area. He walked over to the table where several tomes lay open, the single place where all of those footprints had converged.

In the dim light, he could see that the dust here was light and disturbed; he brought a lantern near to read some of the content. The top book was open to a portrait of a Dragon. Why did this dragon look familiar? He had only ever encountered one.

Johan Dreamed of a human meeting with this Dragon. Her face was the same as the Dragon Angus had slain in Ivonal, but younger. Perhaps an ancestor of this one? Recovering, he read the story of Uvrede the Deposed, and of her great triumphs before the khart failed. He read about her exile to an older island, one covered with only sand and glass.

Some words were foreign - and he realized he was reading an elvish script. Which was odd, because Johan had never even encountered elvish script before. He set that book aside and read the others, coming to a terrible conclusion.

Uvrede was not the ancestor of the Dragon we saw, she WAS that legendary dragon! And someone, some large person, researched her recently right here in the archives! They must have brought her here. I thought I saw a person - an orc? - riding her; but no one was found. So much more to learn...

His thought process was interrupted by a slight shuffling sound from the stacks. At once his sword was in his hand, scanning for the source, determining whether it represented a threat. As it turned out, these were simply the Angels filtering in to join the Bard Corps.

"Old habits die hard," suggested Van, emerging from the stacks. "I was taught to ease into a new place so I could exit easily if needed. Greetings, Ivon Nova."

"Welcome, Van. Welcome all," replied Johan. "Gather, let's find seats and set them in a circle here. We'll be using the space, so stay towards the edges."

He waited for a few moments as the company arranged themselves. When they were all seated, two rows deep, he took a quick count. He was pleased that all of the Angels had chosen to attend. He noted Bram, the grizzled veteran of the Angels who had objected in the last meeting, sitting with a characteristic scowl. The Ivon grabbed the tome with the illustration of Uvrede and strode over to see him.

"Bram, you've inspired me. Your disbelief of dragons in general provides me with the perfect illustration to show the importance of storytelling, and articulate the 'why' behind the Bard Corps."

"If I may." Bram offered, "I've been out to visit the site. I do believe you now."

"Seeing is believing, isn't it? Let me show you something I just learned today." He held up the illustration, showing it to Bram, then walking in a long circle, displaying Uvrede to the whole assembly as he spoke.

"This Dragon is called Uvrede. Uvrede the Deposed. She was the queen of Dragon society roughly ten thousand years ago. This book is a transcription of an earlier work, but I want to hear your observations."

"It looks a lot like our Dragon," Marit suggested.

"Maybe a great, great grandmother?" Cornelia added in.

"Aye," Johan replied, "that's what I thought at first. But then there were the footprints. I had the realization after I swept, but there were recent footprints to this and two other books about dragons, all open to pages about Uvrede. The prints were probably made just a few weeks to a month ago, maybe two."

"Not long before the attack," offered Bram.

"I saw that. And during the attack, I thought I saw a woman, a female orc, riding the dragon." Johan paused as the dots connected in his head. "And the footprints were big, bigger than mine. Like a female orc might have. I think she was right here. I think she researched Uvrede the Deposed.

"She found the name of the island and traveled there. This Dragon wasn't descended from Uvrede. She *was* Uvrede. And Uvrede killed hundreds of Ivonians, and burned a chunk of our city."

He strode dramatically back to the table, placing the book in the same place Zonka had studied it. He turned and walked back to the center of the room, making eye contact with each member of the Bard Corps as he shared his conclusion.

"We didn't know there were dragons. After it came, some of us still had to be convinced. And yet the information sat here in these archives, waiting for someone to find it and understand. In this case, it took an orc to make use of this treasure trove of generational knowledge. An orc.

"Now that we know one example, I ask, what else is hidden here? What do we know that we don't even know that we don't know that we know?"

Listeners winced at the tortured alliteration, even as they realized the gravity of the Ivon's meaning. Johan continued.

"What dangers lurk in these shelves? What cautions can we heed? What can we defend against? What places have we forgotten? How many peoples?

"Conversely, what opportunities are we missing? What treasures are we sitting on unwitting? I fear many. And that leads me to us. Regard yourselves. Regard each other. Ivonia, for generations, had enjoyed a tremendously effective spy network. Our community knows every current event, the prices, and expected prices of each commodity.

"We know who is loyal and who is an agitator. We know so much that can affect our seat of power because we prioritized current events over history. At what cost? We forgot our history, and we are starting to repeat it. It is time, in my estimation, to look inward. To digest and share what we can learn right here in this room.

"After that, we need to reconnect with the rest of the world. My whole life I acted as if the Cyfandir was the bulk of the world. But now I understand how small we are and how insignificant our role is. We need to seek out stories of strangers, of visitors, of people who are different. We need to study them. And we need to explore."

Johan surveyed the assembly, noting their general agreement. Some seemed excited by the idea, some disinterested in change. A few held the fervor and zeal of true devotees, the Ivon Nova paid particular interest to them.

"One of the lost arts that surprised me is a form of dance called Ystyr, or 'Meaning'. I intend to have us all learn it like a second language so we can communicate. Ystyr is a set of movements that can be worked into any physical performance, dancing, singing, and even to a subtle degree, acting or storytelling.[3]

"We will concentrate first on the alphabet, then into words - starting with the most common. Marit, you've shown great dancing skill at the lightplays. Will you assist?"

The company learned the first half of the alphabet in that meeting, ready for another half the next day. By the end of the first, Johan was quite impressed, and excited to see the final result.

---

3 When did the Ivon or even Johan find the time to learn Ystyr? The solution is both complex and simple - they became a part of him in the Dream, while his physical body healed in the Dreamvine. He won't admit to that, of course; much better to look as if he can assimilate knowledge at an unrealistic rate.

Chapter 11

One-Way Ferry

The *Aesig Picil*, or 'Pickle Ferry', steamed quickly across the lagoon, both paddles slapping the water in time. Gierman maintained a steady hand on the rudder as they approached the sandstone cliff where the concealed entrance lay.

He cranked the brakes on the port wheel, throwing the flat-bottomed boat into a sideways slide. When he saw the entrance line up, he threw both levers forward, paddlewheels pulling the water to motivate the vessel. Matching fountains of foamy water launched from the powerful paddles, arcing like a rooster's tail. Gierman smiled. *Those modifications are paying off in smiles per hour, if not miles per hour.*

No goblins stood in his way as he pulled up to the docking station inside. He stepped off and lashed the *Picil* to the dock, the cooling boilers creaking and pinging as hot, expanded metal relaxed. At the end of the dock, he finally met an escort.

A taller goblin, near four-foot tall, hands wringing against each other nervously, strode up stiffly, obviously annoyed.

"Yes? Yes? Well? Yes? Are you going to tell me why you are here, or should I beat it out of you?" His wavering, knock-kneed stance was anything but threatening, but Gierman thought better of laughing outright.

"I wish to register a design! After that, I intend to commission secondary mechanicals." The dwarf had been practicing goblin form and diction. "I think you'll find this interesting."

The goblin tsked and fretted for a moment before stating aggressively, "This way then!" and starting off with a very silly walk.

They proceeded through the old Holt, which Gierman barely recognized. *So many pipes, so many gears, so much metal, so little stone.* After a few hundred feet of twists and turns, the goblin guide poked his head in and nattered at the proprietor. The new goblin popped his head up and assessed.

"Normally I would tell you I was busy, which is true," the engineer said to the dwarf, "but it sounds like you made quite the entrance. From the water! It seems you rattled poor Bazow here."

"Rattled don't enter into it!" Bazow really did appear distressed. "'E washes in here, scarin' the fish and wotnot! 'E's your problem now, and that's an end to it!" The taller goblin stomped off in a huff. The remaining pair smiled after him.

"It's not his fault. He was very near an unexpected explosion back at Seljuk, and he hasn't been the same since. Call me Sergei." The goblin put down the valve he had been adjusting and extended a hand to Gierman. "Tell me about your design, then show me this machine you drove in, Master…"

"Gierman. You'll get a kick out of the *Picil.* And of this," he reached into his bag, producing Alene's pagoda-like toy, "you might find familiar." He handed it over.

"A classic goblin design. You can't register it, of course, as it exists and was built," Sergei paused, assessing the dwarf, "I suspect long before you were born. I had one of these when I was young. Do you want more of these toys to sell?"

"Not exactly. I want to scale this up, and incorporate it into a barge. A powered barge."

Sergei was nonplussed. "Boat? I'll never understand humans and their boats, much less dwarves who take up that odd culture. Why do you want to make this?"

"That is the right question, now isn't it? I have a client who is moving to an island. She wants to run an inn there. The island does not have good building materials, and it sports some aggressive wildlife.

"When we discussed her needs and specifications, we were at a loss for how to make a quickly-built structure that she could occupy. I thought that we might make a barge similar to the *Aesig Picil*, just with paddlewheels at the corners to allow it to make its way to the island, and to drag itself ashore once it arrived.

"But that only got the materials there. We still needed a fast-build time on the structure itself. So Queen Alene, who is a sponsor of this venture, brought out this goblin toy and suggested we might scale it up. Does that seem do-able?"

Sergei thought for a moment. “For most people, no. Too expensive. But if you have a Queen and her budget behind it, perhaps. Show me this boat you propose to base the powerplant on.”

They hustled back to the docks. On the way, Gierman became convinced that Bazow was following them, awkward attempts at stealth sorely lacking. He chuckled. As the *Aesig Picil* came into view, Sergei gasped.

“Beautiful! Brass and gilt ways? I love the design! Is this a goblin ship?”

“I understand it was built by goblins and dwarves together, several hundred years ago. Do you think you could replicate it?”

“Same answer. With deep pockets, yes. But I’ll have to live with it a while to learn it’s workings.”

“This is a working ship. It costs a lot to take it out of service. Why don’t you join me on the next voyage? You can see the incredible work it has to perform.”

“That’s a tough sell.” Sergei considered. “But yes, I think I shall. Let me subcontract some work, and I’ll be ready in a few minutes!”

Chapter 12

At the End of the Day

The front door of the Slumbering Drake was carved like a dragon's mouth, right into the native stone of the cavern that housed the Argentine Holt. Artemus led Floin up the stylized red carpet that led into the pub like a tongue. Floin reached up and tapped a stone dragon's fang as he passed, an action he'd repeated so many times over the roughly five hundred years he'd enjoyed this pub.

Several voices sounded and steins were raised as the two entered, and they took seats at one of Artemus' favorite tables. A middle-aged dwarf with a beard dyed several bright colors skipped up to their table.

"Welcome yer highness! And Master Thunderpick, we're always glad to have you," the dwarf winked, "What can I bring you this afternoon that will increase your smiles?"

"I feel stout today," said the King, "and I'd like to drink one, too. Pick one for me! One with lots of character, like yourself!"

"A great choice, I'm sure! And you, Floin?"

"The same. I trust you!"

The dwarf scurried off to get their drinks, and the dwarves shared a smile. The bard on the stage took their attention for a moment, as he sang a portion of one of Angus' songs.

"Sparks, they flew as he landed, hard nails scarring the stone.
His smile lit with fire, as he thought he'd won.
He approached the Holt, evil glee in his gait,
Ne'er seeing Angus the guard, who lay above in wait.
The Redbeard stood strong, dead-pedaling the gate,
And the new-raised Holtgart earned his place with the greats!"

Floin and Artemus, of course, each knew the real story, but they never discussed it. There was too much at stake to let a misstep derail history. Nor would they discuss it here. Today's meeting had a Purpose. Floin wanted the King's advice.

After their drinks arrived, they ordered big bowls of hearty stew, potatoes, and roasted mushrooms with goat cheese to start. Food that just last year, Floin would have struggled to afford. With his son Angus' success, he no longer had to mine for ore and was quite popular. Sometimes more popular than he was comfortable with.

"Artemus, thank you for taking the time to have dinner with me."

"Of course! I would have come even if you weren't paying. You've been a pleasure of a dwarf to have around, Floin."

"Thank you. I can say it has been an honor to have you as King." Floin took a sip before continuing. "Did you notice what we both did there?"

"We agreed?"

"We did, but we used the past tense. I think," Floin hesitated, "I think my time here might be past. That's what I wanted to talk with you about. Have you ever thought of retiring?"

"Aye," the King nodded, "I have. And more so recently. Those gents back at the Aureate have so much to pass on. I've been thinking of taking time to help them and record their stories before they disappear forever."

"Well, that's noble," Floin stated, "I hadn't gotten to the 'what's next' part. Just thinking it might be time for a change."

"You know I'm six hundred years older than you, right?" The king laughed. "I've had more time to think about it."

"The Aureate, eh?"

"They have plenty of room. And more stories about your son!"

"They would at that, wouldn't they? I've never even been to the Aureate Holt."

"Easily fixed. I intend to go enjoy a spell. Why don't you come with me? Watch my back. Explore the space. Maybe cut loose a little."

"You'd let me join the caravan?"

"No caravan this time. I'll be going alone, or with a friend. Simple travel, just a wagon and supplies. Nothing special."

"You aren't concerned with orcs?"

"No," replied the King with a laugh, "Your son dramatically reduced the numbers to worry about. We haven't heard of any trouble. I suspect they're still licking their proverbial wounds. So, what do you say? Are you in?"

"Wow," said Floin, "imagine a simple miner traveling with a king! I can't say no to that!"

Chapter 13

Finding Out

Zonka broke her fast after a pleasant night in the desert steppes. Today she would reach the Great stone roundhouses that her people would gather in to experience visions - meaningful waking dreams. The visions were seen as divinely inspired messages, especially when one of the wise had one they thought worthy of sharing.

Today was special. Zonka was meeting with a group of the wise, entirely made up of the crones most knowledgeable and valued. Every one was past childbearing age, and considered less distractable, more trustworthy. These meetings came but once a generation.

Zonka thought of her oldest friends; Agatha, C'rin, and Tabitha. They each had traveled hundreds of miles alone to be here, just like her ageless self. Zonka had led their first sweat together, and she knew that this would be the last for Agatha and probably C'rin. They were both already at the end of their natural time.

As she approached the lodge, she saw young Tabitha, merely in her fifties, loading wood into the firepit with two other elders she did not recognize. She climbed the rough stair to stand atop the flat stone roof, which was one massive slab of sandstone. From that perch, she looked east and south, and located the two eldest. Slower than usual, but still present.

Nodding, she descended and greeted the others with a gentle embrace, one at a time. Then she entered the lodge to begin her preparations. She used a bit of her cloak to dust off the stone slab that was her preparatory table. Then she produced several leaves, flowers, and roots of different kinds, laying them out in a ceremonial order. She took the time to re-inspect each for perfection, discarding two leaves that had begun to turn black.

A cauldron was pulled from the fire, the afternoon's stew finished - at least the mundane elements. Meat and vegetables, pleasantly spiced. Zonka processed her finishing touches, bringing some whole leaves and some carefully bruised to release their medicines completely.

"Welcome, friends," she said without looking, knowing from the sounds and the presences that her friends had arrived. 'Let us begin."

The other elders filed up to Black Zonka, the oldest orc in history, each holding their own bowl. Each bowl was different; some carved from wood, some ceramic masterpieces, and Agatha's worked from the remains of a bear skull[4]. The oldest two shared a knowing smile as they remembered.

The group took places around the fire, several adding cushions for comfort. Zonka used no cushion. Her place had indentations that matched her hips perfectly, worn in from literally thousands of sweats. They ate in silence, then meditated in place as the fire continued to heat the space. They made a music, a droning resonance, that passed through several octaves as they prepared for hours in the same place.

----- -----

Indaria broke the connection to the Dreamvine by removing her hand from the smaller pod. She was here and aware, awake; she had learned many things about Dreamvines, and how to use them. She reached over and tapped Endaria, her father and Speaker for the woodland elves, on the shoulder. He responded by breaking contact, and the two walked down steps that led away from the sacred pool of Sara-Tholah and into the woods.

"Do you see it now?" asked Indaria lo Thenalah to her father.

"I'm impressed at your control," he responded. "You have increased your mastery over plants considerably."

"That's not what I'm talking about and you know it."

"You mean the orc?"

4 Agatha was very attached to her bear skull bowl. Not only had she used her craft to shape it, but she had slain the bear. In single combat. Unarmed. Agatha was not a person to be trifled with, even at her advanced age.

"Yes. Do you see how we, the Dreamvine and myself, can reshape her? Make her into a force for good?"

"You flatter yourself," said the older elf. "You cannot change a person with dreams. You might help them practice one aspect of their personality, but nothing more."

"What evil did you see in that ceremony?" Indaria 's frustration showed in furrowed brows and pursed lips.

"None. There is nothing evil in the ceremony itself. Nor is there evil in Zonka. She has always wanted the best for her people."

"Yes. But I think we can use the dreams of generations to educate her about other peoples. To bring in other points of view. To help her empathize with non-orcs."

The Speaker sighed. "I can't stop you. I won't stop you. But Zonka isn't what I'm really worried about."

She stepped back, suspicious. "What worries you, father?"

"Le'el."

"And what is that?"

"You don't know yet? I'm surprised, given everything that has occurred." The Speaker tilted his head thoughtfully. "And then again, I am not."

"What is Le'el, father?" Indaria's voice was fierce, bordering on threatening. "Tell me."

"I cannot."

"Tell. Me."

"I cannot tell you what Le'el is, because he is a person. Was a person. He became something entirely different."

"Who, then?"

"Le'el is the elf who joined the Dreamvine so many millennia ago. Long before even my time."

Indaria visibly struggled with the concept. *It explains so much, but opens so many more questions! Was that the presence I felt chased by? The warm spot near me when I woke?*

"How do you know this?" she demanded.

"As I said, your mastery over plants and magic is growing greatly. But you still have a lot to learn. A lot to learn."

----- -----

As Tabitha finished describing her experience, Agatha choked. The old orc, whom Zonka had known her entire eighty-four years, locked eyes with Zonka and started to convulse. Sweat beaded on her brow, then poured off in sheets.

"Ack," Agatha tried to speak, but bloody foam came out instead.

Zonka knew what was happening, and exactly which poisonous herb had this effect. She must have made a mistake with the hallucinogenic mixture. *But if I made the mistake, it will happen to all of them. All of us. And there is no cure, no antidote.*

She looked around, every one of her sisters in various stages of poisoning. She could feel the effects starting in her body, too; but it would not be soon enough. She watched them all die as the pain started to wrap her in its fatal embrace...

----- -----

"Le'el." Indaria thought the name into the handpod she engaged. *"That is your name, Le'el, is it not?"*

Indaria searched for Zonka's presence. She found her in a dreamless sleep, with an elevated heart rate. The orc's wounds were nearly healed, with fewer and fewer tendrils supporting her in the pod.

"What have you done to her?" Indaria demanded.

"She sleeps," came the reply. *"Dreamless sleep now, her dream had come to its conclusion. I have added it to the library. Come inside again, and I will show it to you."*

Chapter 14

Falling Ahead

Autumn fell from the heights of summer, and time passed. The Cyfandir was a peaceful place entirely for a time, and the chaos of the last several months left people with a greater appreciation for gentle words and forward foci.

The Ivon Nova's Angels largely transitioned into the Bard Corps, with a few choosing to retire into more sedentary roles within the government, and several leaving the service altogether to enjoy the spoils of decades of dishonesty. Those that advanced learned the dance-like language of Ystyr.

They uncovered treasure troves of stories, and designed efficient systems to teach and learn stories, songs and dances. Every bit of Johan's vision unfolded as he set out, yet he was never satisfied. He insisted that they push harder every day, training like elite athletes.

The rest of Ivonia worked diligently to repair the damage from the battle and the dragon's attack. Several buildings had been completely lost, and sections of the cobbled road had to be replaced. Wherever possible, Johan directed, the damage should be memorialized; the people would remember what brought them together.

Gymdeithas Fasnach thrived. New trade routes were established, and Patrick's efforts paid off for the community. Repairs and rebuilding of the Greenway finished up, and the Spring wheat crops flourished. Life, for the moment, was good under this new self-rule.

So it was at Canolbwynt Masnach. Docks rebuilt, and more than half the town was starting anew. The mysterious trees that Bedwyn advised a reverence towards grew strong and tall at a pace that seemed wholly unnatural.

Nearby in the new goblin outpost of Cam Makinesi business reigned supreme. While the majority of their efforts went to making the old dwarven holt suitable for goblin use, several major projects advanced. Brin's mobility device, Gierman's expanding barge house, and the prospect of a new fleet of steam wagons had the pumps fully primed.

The Veyns enjoyed increased trade and lowered anxiety with the most major threat neutralized and apparently an ally. The dwarves' marble foundations allowed for new building projects for the first time in three hundred years. Alene was ecstatic to see the success of her people.

One of the challenges that seemed to limit potential expansion was simply the lack of trading partners. Traders knew that there were more possibilities to the south, but the Winding that ran from west to east hundreds of miles south was effectively impenetrable. Only a select few knew how to traverse the Winding, and they never let on that they had any clue.

One of the fabled places lost to the Winding was Mirekka. The Bard Corps had discovered a number of old songs about Mirekka, many of which included dragons. The Mirekkans were the arbiters of peace and justice throughout the world, according to some accounts. The most far-fetched suggested that they controlled dragons!

All told, it was an excellent run until the end of fall, when things started getting interesting again…

Chapter 15

Shameless Self-Promotion

A young man of seventeen years sat quietly in the tavern he knew he was too young to attend. He shouldn't even be in the Dives; an enclave of bars, brothels and warehouses, all of ill repute. This was one part of the city that did a good job of self-policing and keeping minors out. This minor danced a razor's edge that made it believable he was of age.

He nursed a foamy beer and a bowl of chips, listening to the rough-and-tumble bard entertain a rough-and-tumble crowd. He brushed sandy-blonde hair out of the way of his ear to hear better. Not to hear the bard, but the low tones and whispers of the neighboring table.

"All is in place," said the one in clean, white clothes quietly. "I've me and the missus all hired and domestic-like."

"Is one of you in the kitchen?"

"As you asked, yeah. I'm in and out several times a day, and she's baking non-stop."

The man in the heavy leather coat produced a vial of liquid. "This can go onto the salad, after the taster has passed the food. That gives us the first several hours of the night to get in and out."

"Is there any chance this will hurt them?"

"There's always a chance," replied leather jacket, "but do you care? For the money involved, you won't have to worry about anything ever again!"

The table was jostled as a drunk slammed against it, spilling several drinks.

"Oi! Watch it!" shouted the clean man.

Jacket put a hand on the domestic's shoulder. "No need for that. Here, youngster, take this bread. It'll soak up some of that rotgut."

The youth smiled and raised the loaf to his mouth, covering his face as he stumbled toward the stairs. He checked the vial he had palmed and smiled as he secured it. He was on the third step, still staggering, when the shouts took up again.

"Stop! Thief!"

"'Ere, you've got a pickpocket in yer bar," said the domestic to the man behind the counter."

"In a place like this? Couldn't be! I'll call the coppers for you, shall I?" The proprietor chuckled. "He's getting away..."

The domestic followed Jacket and their quarry up the stairs to the blue-tiled roof four floors above. The youth was at the end of the widow's walk, a small, railed path at the peak of the roof.

"Give me the vial and this will be easier for you, kid."

"And what if I don't?" came the rebellious answer.

"Then," Jacket said as he moved the long side of his coat aside, revealing a quick sword, "we go the hard way. Trust me, you want the easy way."

The youth looked over his shoulder at the roof and inevitable fall below. There was not much to slow a descent. He hopped his butt up onto the railing and said simply, "I guess you got me."

Jacket smiled and closed the distance with long, confident strides. The youth, without changing his expression in the slightest, leaned back to fall headfirst on the slick, blue, ceramic tiles. He slid on his cloak, gaining speed downward. Right before the edge, he reached his arms over his shoulders and grabbed the tiles with his palms, rolling up into a handstand.

From his handstand the youth sighted a laundry line just under the eave. He kicked with his legs as he pressed up, hopping off the roof headfirst. He reached for the line, which held his weight as his body swiveled down. As his feet hit their lowest point, he pulled hard on the line above, freeing rusty bolts from the building he had just left.

A half second later, he was swinging downward in a tight arc that he calculated would land him on the wall painfully. Instead he aimed for a window below the wall, releasing the line at what he desperately hoped was the right moment. It was, and his feet crashed through shutters and windowpane, bringing him inside a room on the second floor.

As he rolled to a stop and stood up, he tried to make sense of what he was seeing. Maps on every wall surface all around the room showed locations that the young man knew to be here in Ivonal, plus others he did not recognize. Pins with names were placed in many spots on these maps. A list of corresponding names was plastered to one wall.

The door at one end of the room opened, and a woman of great beauty stepped out. She looked at the youth, the window, and the walls, realization dawning even as the intruder ran out the far door. She pursued.

While the runner did not know every map, he did know this place well. He sprinted two buildings down, jumping to run on the far wall of the alleyway in order to execute a lightspeed turn. He ran for a moment looking back to see if he had shaken his pursuers when he crashed right into two men, knocking them to the ground with the force of a tackle.

A sack of something powdered flew from their hands, broke apart, and covered the alley in white. The downed men shouted with suspicion and drew weapons as the youth rolled over his shoulder and continued his cross-alley sprint. A third man raced after him.

He emerged into the next street in time to see his newest pursuer and the woman with the maps running fast down the alley behind him. A glance to the side revealed Jacket, who continued his pursuit. The fugitive parsed what he knew about the area and decided to run into the backstage area of the Palace of Lights.

Despite the name, the Palace of Lights would be dark at this hour of the afternoon, and largely empty. Add in the plethora of passageways and curtains, and he was sure to escape there. Two blocks later, he turned into the alleyway where supplies and sets were loaded from wagons. He sprinted up the steps and grabbed the doorhandle - locked.

Three pairs of feet slowed to a walk and cornered him. *Maybe they are from rival factions,* he desperately hoped. His hope faded as they spoke.

"This one is mine, I don't need help," the woman spoke first. "I just want to find out what he saw."

"You can talk to him after I get my pound of flesh," growled alleyway. "Two years of investigation to get to that deal, and he's blown the evidence across half the town."

"This kid stole from me. I'll take my property back, give him a few lashes, then you lot can argue over him!"

What are the odds that these people all know each other? The youth thought. *Three sets of criminals doing different things so close together? Unless they aren't criminals...*

"You are all cops!" he shouted.

The three smiled at each other.

"You should be so lucky," said map-woman.

"Cops have rules they have to follow." Jacket looked like he was enjoying this.

The youth realized the truth only a half-second later.

"You are all Angels! The Ivon's personal agents!"

A clear voice came from above.

"An astute observation." The Ivon applauded from a balcony thirty feet above. "Not one a person should usually admit to knowing." He faced the pursuers - Angels - and continued. "How did this happen? How did three of my best get made by a youth who nearly eluded all three?"

"He pretended to be a drunkard and palmed a valuable vial. I had to give chase. My character would never allow a theft to go unpunished," said Jacket.

"And yet, Brennan," said the Ivon, "here he stands, apparently unpunished. Again I ask, how?"

"Either he is the best acrobat I've ever seen, or the luckiest hoodrat. I had a hard time tracking him."

"Were you working with Martina? I see her panting, defeated, as well."

"I still don't know how, but this little bugger blasted right through shuttered windows and saw some sensitive information. I had to find out what he knew before I could take care of him."

The Ivon's gaze fell upon the young man, apparently winded as he leaned on the locked door.

"And you've neither learned what he knows nor taken care of him." The Ivon shifted his gaze to the other male pursuer. "And your story, big-man-I-don't-know?"

"Mak, yer highness. It's an honor. I've been deep undercover for two years, and this street thug blew the whole operation. I may never gain their trust again."

The Ivon looked down at the youth again, who squirmed uncomfortably against the door frame.

"What is your name, boy? Don't bother lying, I'll know soon enough."

"Johan. Johan C'Antrell."

"I see. Nobility, misbehaving? I can't imagine. What am I to do with a fish too small to make a meal of, and one too big to throw back?"

"Keep fishing!" The young Johan shouted, as he finished picking the lock behind his back. He fled into the building, chased by his pursuer's curses and the Ivon's laughter.

----- -----

Johan C'Antrell, Ivon Nova, brought himself back to the present. He leaned on the marble banister of his southern balcony, surveying all that he was now responsible for. The Dives were less than one percent of his domain, yet he found himself reminiscing nearly every time his gaze ran across them.

If it hadn't been for his daring escape and a chance meeting with the Ivon Prior, he wouldn't be here. Even if the Ivon Prior had fallen in battle or even been toasted by Uvrede's fiery visit, the great Houses of Ivonia would still be fighting over the title. Nobles were rarely as 'noble' as they let on.

Here he stood, the most powerful man in the Cyfandir, afforded every luxury he desired, respected by his people, at peace with the other factions, and he was unhappy. While he was built for this, the change left him feeling isolated.

Luxury was wonderful, but it was the action, the risk, the grit that made Johan feel the most alive. In his decade with the Angels, his accomplishments already put him in the conversation with the best and brightest of an already exclusive group. That part of his life was done.

Every day - several times each day - he considered disappearing. Traveling the world. The wider world, far beyond these constricting Cyfandric borders. Not an aimless travel, either. Now that he had seen Uvrede, watched her power, seen the fragility of an entity thousands of years old, he wanted to know more.

Learning more meant finding two places: Shurakhame, the legendary capital of dragonkind. The archives had yielded no first-hand accounts, only stories retold many times before being written down. That always bothered Johan. It felt unreliable.

The other was Mirekka. Many accounts of Mirekka were easily found in the Archives, including a location - an impossible location. Mirekka was right on the Winding line, doomed to exist in the eternal storm. Mirekkans, in most accounts, were a just and honorable people. They were relied upon to settle disputes and dissuade war, in some accounts worldwide.

They could do this, it was said, because of their connection with dragons. Not Dragons like Uvrede, at least not commonly. Younger Dragons. Smaller Dragons. That was a puzzle Johan had not uncovered yet. This unsolved riddle burned inside him. He needed to know.

He looked over the docks at the rebuilding. Months in, with colder weather on the way, the Grand Harbor was once again a functioning port. Much of the navy was in serviceable condition, if not near its former glory. The *Hidden Queen* had not returned yet, and he worried for the crew.

He skated his eyes from the western heights to the eastern wall, taking in several hundred thousand souls. He worried for them all. And that was the problem. When he was merely worried about his own safety, the world was an easier, more enjoyable place.

He returned to his chambers a prisoner of his own privilege and power. There was much to do. He saw Ynghild step gracefully in from the northern balcony, all poise and allure.

"Semaphore from the Northgate. Patrick has arrived."

"Has he? Excellent. Send him to the Harbor. I'll meet him there."

Chapter 16

Does This Smell OK to You?

Patrick stepped out onto the open plaza that serviced the Grand Harbor. Large warehouses sacrificed their frontage to house small shops, the kind of place one might find great prices on goods that didn't make it to the fanciest stores in Ivonal.

He had already turned down three of the street peddlers when a grubby fisherman who reeked of shellfish approached. A wide-brimmed hat hid his face.

"A fishing tour of the harbor interests you? Mmm?" The voice had a tenor warble to it, the grammar disastrous.

"No, thank you," replied the burly smith. "I am supposed to meet someone here."

"Meet someone? Mmmhmm!" the fisherman continued, bemused. "Met someone you have!" The man placed a fishy, gloved hand on Patrick's arm.

Patrick recoiled in disgust, having already bathed to be sure not to insult the Ivon. "No thank you. This is a person of importance. A politician."

"Important Politician, ooh! Politics not make one important."

"Look, I've had just about enough of you!"

"And here I thought we hadn't even begun." Johan lifted the brim of his hat enough for Patrick to see. "Come, embark we must! Special fish there are!" He trotted off down the docks, giggling loudly as he ran to a fifteen-foot-long rowboat.

Patrick stood dumbfounded for a moment before shaking his head and following.

Johan kept up the act until they were past the seawall, where no one would be able to hear them.

"Thanks for coming out. Sorry about the smell."

"Are you kidding me? I love fishing! I haven't had the time for months with all of this diplomacy crap."

"I hear that," said Johan through a big smile. "Leadership isn't all it's cracked up to be."

"Leadership? Is that what we're calling this?" Patrick cut bait and prepped a hook. "Seems like more of a vacation."

"You've got to stop to smell the roses or you'll forget what they are." Johan responded while he readied a rod.

"That's a good point. But from my seat, you don't smell like roses."

"Ha! True, and it cost me a day's worth of fisherman's wages to buy this from an old man coming in. I wanted the authenticity. If my bodyguards find me out here, they'll flip."

"Bodyguards. Ugh." Patrick cast his line. "What is that like? Do you really need them?"

"Not yet," replied Johan, "but I suspect it is a matter of time. Every time a place changes leadership, some ambitious young soul will try to press their advantage. I know I would."

"Yet you aren't worried about me? I outweigh you by thirty stone."

"If I thought you had an ounce of guile in you, Patrick, we wouldn't be on this boat together. But you don't, and we are. So, let's catch up. How are things with Gymdeithas Fasnach?"

"Remarkably well, thanks. Your quick action with reparations and help have gone a long way to smoothing out the Ivon Prior's crimes. Under the right conditions, you might get control back."

"If I wanted control. I don't."

"Why not?"

"Too much trouble! As long as you keep that machine rolling well, there is no profit in my trying to run things. I have enough to worry about."

"Like fishing?"

"Fishing like this?" Johan gestured. "Absolutely! What could be more important than a one-on-one meeting with the Head of State for the community that surrounds Ivonia?"

Patrick nodded.

"We aren't across the river."

"Indeed. Who, do you suppose, is?"

"Some stories say it is haunted. Others, that it is riddled with orcs. In either case, we stay on our side of the river, and we have no problems."

"What would you say to this?" Johan asked. "We send emissaries, jointly, to explore and ask."

"I would be honored by the suggestion. Then I would politely decline. Gymdeithas Fasnach has too much to do in our already spread out lands. While we might welcome others, we have to focus inward before expanding."

Patrick's line jiggled, and they were silent while he manipulated the rod, setting the hook. Several minutes later, a fat flounder settled into the bucket.

"That looks like lunch," Patrick offered.

"Let's get another first. I'm enjoying this."

"That makes one of us," Patrick lamented. "I was drafted into this role, and I can't see a way out. Who knew anarchic self-determination would be so complex?"

"I did."

"Prick."

"Why," Johan mocked with false outrage, "would you say a thing like that?"

"We went over this. I know you initiated Gymdeithas Fasnach. If you knew it would be a pain in the ass, why sell everyone on the concept?"

"It had to be done. The Ivon Prior had become dangerous and unpredictable. After Pentref, I saw no choice. And there wouldn't be a better moment to start."

Patrick stifled a grimace.

"I was there. I've never been so motivated."

"Exactly. That heart-pain is what it takes to make a nation rise up. The Ivon Prior was only vulnerable a short time. I had to do something, and that is what I could come up with on short notice."

"At least you admit it."

"I'll deny it to my dying day. But you've seen through me, Patrick. So here, in this very private, exclusive environment, I'll let on. You would be wise to keep this to yourself. If it gets out, you will find unrest sooner."

A second flounder soon found its way up and into the bucket, and the two returned to shore. Patrick left on foot to find the inn

Johan sponsored, and The Ivon Nova, the most powerful man in a thousand miles, walked in through the service entrance wearing rags and stinking of shellfish.

Chapter 17

The Stacks

After a good bath and a fine dinner of flounder with fried tates from the Greenway, Johan sent Patrick on his way. He selected his old standby from the closet, a bright red-and-gold doublet with puffy sleeves that he used in his days as a bard. Since this evening was to be filled with outlining the light play for the winter festival, he hoped it would bring inspiration.

To that end, he eschewed the formal stairs for some of the back-ways and hidden passages he'd used as an Angel. Rappelling down the shaft that paralleled the stairs was exhilarating as always, and it allowed him to slip away from his bodyguards for the second time that day.

Two miles of needlessly twisted and obscured paths later, he arrived at his destination. He walked up the marble steps (dwarven work, Angus had shared with him) and up to the massive, dark-stained oak doors. He reached up and raised the large iron ring on the left-hand door, then dropped it against the clacker[5], a loud clap echoing through the gathering evening.

Though Johan could not hear the footsteps approaching, he knew they were there. A small hatch opened in the door below the knocker, a cherubic face showing a smile before it was slapped shut again. The Librarian opened the small man-gate that was inset into the larger structure and bid him enter.

"Ivon Nova, we welcome you! Later than usual. How can we serve?" Janet the Librarian was a woman in her sixties with a pleasantly plump look. She was always dressed impeccably, no matter what time of day or night the Ivon visited.

---

5 This ring was twelve inches across, housed in the mouth of a dragon. The clacker plate was formed by what appeared to be metallic feathers on the dragon's neck, drawn down to points. There was a story behind this, a large and powerful one. Something that none of the Bard Corps, not even Johan, had figured out yet; despite operating it daily for weeks.

"Madame Librarian, it is a pleasure to see you! I'm headed to the Archives for a little research and writing. I don't think I should bother you this late at night." Johan had to duck to enter, the gate having been made for a time when Ivonians were shorter.

"Late at night, he says! Pish!" She looked out at the gathering twilight as she closed the door. "It isn't even full dark yet!" When the door shut, the lantern in her hand was the only light in the large atrium.

"Is there anything I can get you?" she continued.

"Candles, perhaps. A lantern or two. That would be very helpful, thank you."

She had already begun to light a second lantern for him, sharing the flame with a small bit of paper rolled up. She led him down the familiar hallway to the stairs, downward and to the rear of the building.

The Archives were unlike any other building that Johan had experienced. Older. Grander. They were formed from granite and marble, with lofty arches dozens of feet above. Woods and inlays and patterns were populated throughout. One of these inlays was set into the floor of the archival room, a life-sized representation of the city of Ivonal and the land surrounding. The perfect place to think through how to structure the story of the city's fiery upheaval and the new entity that rose up from the ashes like a phoenix.

Janet left the hall after setting enough candles and lanterns to light the hall to a dim level. Johan dragged chairs and tables out of the way, leaving one that was about the size of the Theater of Lights near the center of the city on the map. He settled this over the spot, propping the legs on books to affect a standing desk. He unrolled the sheaf of paper he'd brought, with quills and ink and pounce pot, onto the desk.

Once everything was prepared, he quickly got to the task of… pacing. He walked here and there, looking at the points on the map-floor that he'd be highlighting. As he realized the complexity, he strode over to a chalkboard that stood ready at the side and grabbed several colors. These he took from place to place, making notes on the floor surface itself.

He traced the movements of the Ivonian troops. Marked out the combined forces of Gymdeithas Fasnach. He showed how the Smaragdine dwarves came in when the Ivonian cavalry was chased out by Uvrede. But he did change how he and Alene and Ynghild had entered; as he also skipped over how the Argentine dwarves accessed the city center without being stopped.

Uvrede he marked with yellow and red, indicating the places she had set homes and businesses ablaze. Swirling marks showed the movement of troops, with small statues standing in for the events in the Ivon's tower shown on the tower. All of the facts and figures, set and ready for transformation into a great lightplay.

He took a break to sneak outside for a late snack and found that some of the pubs had closed already. But as he moved towards the docks, where activity lingered well into the night, he was able to secure a beer and rushed sausages and chips. There was a time when he might have turned his nose up at subpar food, but the char on the meat and too-dark hue in the chips fed his creativity tonight. Exactly what he needed.

He marked the stars and moon above as he strolled openly back to the library. Bats fluttered to and fro, their travel marked when the lights were momentarily blocked. *That is how I'll introduce the dragon,* he thought. *But I must call her by her name, Uvrede. Most people have no idea of the import of her arrival and her passing; I have to convey that. And Dragon, as big of a term as that is, says nothing of her truth, her age, her meaning.*

He worked for hours more, plotting and planning, drawing out the story and making notes for ways to show it in the lightplay format. His night swam with words and blocking and stage directions. Page by page, line by line, the Lightplay formed.

He was awakened by a gentle, soft hand on his shoulder. Janet stood over him with a glass of cool water while he slumped in the chair. She offered a healthy breakfast and asked him about his process - he was happy to explain. It was near noon when they parted, Johan heading off to deal with affairs of state, Janet assuring him that his space would be held in stasis until he returned.

Janet had learned a lot, which left her yearning for more. She spent some time in her quarters, thinking things through as she painted nesting dolls on her day off.

Chapter 18

What Goes Around

Bills paid, Brin watched the young groom lash the mule to the wagon. He'd have to do these things himself, no matter how difficult it might be. He offered a large tip and practiced the process several times.

Loaded with supplies and garden seeds, Brin headed north. A few miles north of town, he steered the wagon to the forest's edge and tied the mule up. He made his way in with a shovel as his crutch.

He was looking for a depression in the earth where nefarious deeds had occurred several months back. Stolen gold had been buried here, along with three corpses.[6]

He found the depression, and indeed the earth was still disturbed - but not at all like before!

Clods of dried mud and dead grass were splattered on all of the neighboring trees, rocks, and bushes. Almost as if there had been an explosion. The place where Brennan had buried the gold and the bodies would have been higher than this deeper place. More concerning was the arrow-straight tillage that led northwest.

It looked as if dozens of farmers had crisscrossed the ground with dozens of plows - perfectly tilled, with clover and grass starts attesting that this was also at least a few weeks back. Brin spoke out loud. To himself? To the mule? It hardly mattered anymore.

"How dare someone steal the gold I stole from the man who stole it from Veynsport?" He laughed out loud as he realized the sheer ridiculousness of his complaint.

"Whatever did that, I don't want to know. Terrifying."

---

6 Three corpses, but only two heads. The third was too valuable to leave and had been recovered not long after being buried. Like its former owner, the face had been no more obnoxious dead than when it was alive. DePet was not remembered with fondness.

He returned to his wagon and drove the mule north along the road for several days. Eventually he reached the north side of the mountains, where his journey would become harder.

He spent a whole day maneuvering to different hilltops to study the mountain, charting possible routes to the top. He never spotted his target, the goblin flyer's workshop, but he had a reasonable idea of where it should be. That evening he spent his time deciding on tomorrow's route.

He started early, not much after sunrise. The mule was sure-footed, and the two-wheeled wagon small enough to not encumber it badly. They climbed until mid-day, when Brin called for a break and shuffled his way to a rock outcropping that afforded a better vantage point.

For the first time, he sighted the workshop. It was right where he supposed it to be, and better yet, there was a route to the shop that made for easy travel. Before nightfall he was unloading his gear from the wagon and setting a high line for the mule to graze from.

While the sun disappeared, Brin felt a great deal of accomplishment. But after he closed his eyes, he was once again haunted by the ghosts that he knew as Brennan lay below.

Chapter 19

Is That a Building in Your Pocket?

"Sergei!" Bazow shouted in a shrill Voice. "Sergei, there is a dwarf here to see you! A fat one at that! Perhaps you should come out and prevent him from eating anything of ours - or everything of ours!" The skinny goblin looked Gierman up and down with blatant disapproval.

"You've got no respect for the value of a good dwarven meal, I see."

"'Respect?' That's down the hall. I'm 'Pointing out the Obvious!'" With that, Bazow strode away, his walk even sillier than before.

As if on cue, Sergei appeared from around a corner, wiping bearing grease off of his hands with a grease-soaked rag. Ineffectual, but very on-brand.

"Gierman!" he laughed. "So nice to see you! I've been testing your mechanism; would you like to see it?"

"Aye, that'd be great," replied the dwarf, "But I wonder, is your friend Bazow all right? He's always so… tightly wound."

"What, that? Now that's very loose indeed for Bazow. Sometimes he can come across a bit abrasive. Not all gentle like this evening."

Gierman followed Sergei, head shaking, through several passages until they reached a tall, airy chamber that housed a mess of iron girders on the floor in the middle.

"Well?" Sergei was proud. "Exactly to your spec. I figure it is better than you hoped, yes?"

Gierman took a moment to take it all in. There was no space inside for- for anything, really. Way too dense to float. And the

GREASE! Every surface, every edge, coated in a quarter of an inch of grease.

"I have to say," said Gierman, "I am a bit surprised. Did we specify grease?"

"You said it had to survive an ocean crossing. The grease will keep the salt water out. I was proud of that addition…"

"All right, I can understand that. Is this the whole thing, or will you add more floors above?"

"You don't see the…" Sergei began, "Oh, never mind. Let me show you how it works."

Sergei worked his way into the tangled nest of iron beams, copper wiring, and brass fittings, grunting and leaning in ways that were tight even for a slightly-built goblin like himself. It would be difficult for most dwarves and humans, and impossible with Gierman's increased girth.

Five minutes in, Gierman peered through the complex contraption, barely making out Sergei's movements near the exact center. He seemed to be fiddling with knobs and levers, muttering to himself, and stoking a fire. Smoke billowed out of the low stacks, filling the chamber and making it difficult to breathe. Then the humming started.

Low tones and vibrations at first, rising higher in time. At several frequencies the machine would rattle and shake, smoothing out until the next disturbing harmonic. Eventually the sound was a simple, stable, high-pitched whine. For the first time in ten minutes, Sergei called out.

"Stand clear! If it gets ya, it's yer own fault!"

Gierman indeed took several steps back. From the perimeter of the frame, heavy, flat feet stomped out and smashed into the floor. The outer wall became very solid. Then a sound of a flywheel engaging a secondary machine through a very loud clutch, and the entire internal frame rose, slowly, until it affected a second floor.

Automatic latches threw themselves as the whine rose again, then the same loud clutch engaged. A frame inside the outermost rose, faster than the first, making a smaller third story. This process repeated two more times, stopping just inside the roughly fifty-foot-tall ceiling. When the final latches were in place, Sergei proudly stepped out from the skeleton of a mid-sized building.

"Well?" He asked, beaming, "What do you think?"

"I love the finished product. I'm sure Beatrice will be happy. But you've painted yourself into a corner, Sergei."

"No paint. Grease. S'better."

"A figure of speech. You've built yourself into the machine until it is installed. None of us are small enough to make it happen!"

The boffin took a moment to consider.

"The price goes up. I'll need an extra two percent per day."

"Done. Now let's get this deflated and loaded onto the *Picil*."

The process of undoing the building was considerably slower, as Sergei had to maneuver to each lock and release it. Two hours later, the folded assembly was wheeled over to the *Aesig Picil* and loaded aboard. It was near the capacity of the stone-carrying ship, but they made do.

At one point, Sergei slipped on a greased beam and went into the water. Gierman grabbed his belt with a boathook and hauled the goblin to safety.

"Are you still sure grease is better?" jibed Gierman.

"Definitely. If that beam hadn't been greased, I might have hurt myself instead of slipping!"

Chapter 20

A Line in the Sand

"This makes no sense," Laurent fretted. "We made these slipways to launch ships, not haul equipment. All of this iron - it must weigh a ton!"

"Seventeen." Gierman was matter-of-fact about the challenging task. "But I'm excited to see how we'll float it up!"

The dwarf had grounded the *Aesig Picil* sideways on the lower portion of the slipway at high tide, and waited 'til low tide to offload Beatrice's new home frame. Now three dozen men levered, hauled, greased ways, and ran winches to move this gigantic metal contraption up into the shipyard.[7]

It took four hours, but they eventually had the frame on land and secured to the two dollies they used to maneuver it around the shipyard. Once it was in the center of the yard, they walked around it in wonder, trying to make heads or tails of the goblins' work.

Sergei finally felt comfortable approaching. His passage across the lagoon had been unpleasant, to say the least. Now he was no longer several seasick shades of purple and blue, and walked steadily.

Laurent brought over a large blackboard with multiple colors of chalk. And they talked, and they drew, and they talked, and they drew. What follows are merely snippets of their conversation.

"This is the front, correct?"
"If you want to sail strictly sideways, yes."
(sighing) "Which way is the front?"

---

7 During this process, Gierman noted the human's noses wrinkling near the sweaty form of Sergei. Goblin bathing standards were opposite Veynsian expectations. So Gierman watched for an opportunity and conveniently lost his hold on a line at the right moment for Sergei to find himself in the drink again. The smells of brackish water and seaweed were much more to the shipyard worker's liking.

"Sergei, how will the paddlewheels be powered?"

"We've set power take-offs at the sides, here, and… here."

"So we can power two paddlewheels. Do they have individual power for differential steering?"

"Exactly, just like the *Aesig Picil.*"

"How are we getting this up onto land at the destination? Are there slipways?"

"I guess we'll have to build some."

"There is no straight-grained wood on the island. That would be problematic."

"Too bad we can't have a wheeled cart like these to roll it right up the sand."

"Why not? We'll have the paddlewheels for power."

"The paddlewheels are centered."

"Do they have to be?"

All three considered this in silence.

"No."

"If we split the power to a pair of paddlewheels at the front and another pair at the rear…"

"...it could crawl right up the beach!"

"We have to anchor it against the storms, which can be powerful."

"It has feet."

"They might sink into the sand."

"Can we drive pylons into the feet to anchor them?"

"Elegant!"

They went on like this for hours, each offering ideas and analyzing merits. Eventually they had a well-engineered plan that covered flotation, landing, and expansion. The question of how they could accomplish this unheard-of feat was covered. The team were congratulating themselves with a lunch of vinegared tomatoes and fresh, stringy cheese when Beatrice arrived.

"Good afternoon, gents. I hear you've made progress."

"We have, ma'am," answered Gierman.

She stood in front of the mass of machinery and asked, "Where is it?"

"Right here!" Sergei stepped over and caressed an iron girder proudly. "Isn't it beautiful?"

"Urggh…" Beatrice began, "I don't think I'll fit in there. It is all machine!"

"Aha! You haven't seen its party trick!" Sergei dropped onto a wheeled creeper and rolled along under the monstrosity (which was elevated on shipyard trolleys, leaving just enough room for a goblin to maneuver). When he reached the control room in the center, he stood.

A series of clanks, clatters, and screeches marked the starting of the steam engine at its heart. The fire had been burning for a while now, most of a full head of steam built up while they sat. Sergei threw the right series of levers, and several floors rose, one at a time. When it clanged to a stop, Sergei threw the locks and walked confidently out of the control room, arms spread wide to indicate the space.

"Oh," responded the older woman, "it is a lot of space, now, isn't it? Will there be - and I'm spitballing here - walls? Floors? Ceilings?"

"But of course!" Laurent was by her side, patting her on the shoulders to ease her worry. "Now that we have the structure, you can instruct us how you would like it to look. This is the skeleton, you will tell us how the flesh works around it."

"I see."

"There will be some constraints, mainly weight, and some provisions for joints. But after seeing how this works, I am confident that we can make you happy. Come, let us draw out some possibilities…"

Laurent led Beatrice away from the beaming Sergei and chuckling Gierman. He took her to the room where shipbuilders designed trade ships, complete with a talented artist and veteran shipbuilders. Beatrice composed herself well for a person who was introduced to her forever home in the form of a greased metal contraption that unfolded.

Chapter 21

On Mirekka

"It's time, Ivon." Ynghild was perfectly put together, every hair in place around her delicate tiara. Coupled with her deep-blue gossamer dress, she looked ready to be a queen. More than appropriate for her duties as the Ivon Nova's second-in-command.

"Can it wait?" Johan, the Ivon Nova, most powerful man on the Cyfandir, leaned over a long table covered with books, scrolls, and sheafs of paper. His hair was mussed, wearing a robe and one slipper. A quill stuck over his ear dripped ink onto his shoulder. "I have a lot to do here."

"The Council awaits. As important as the Lightplay is, running the country must take priority." Ynghild opened the closet and selected an outfit, all blues with silver trim. She laid the clothes on the bed and walked towards the door. "I'll send lunch. You need to get ready. Five minutes."

Johan dressed like a petulant child. He splashed water from a pitcher into his basin, washed his face and slicked back his hair. He had his shoes on just as Ynghild opened the door again without knocking. She held a large stuffed and fried egg-noodle roll wrapped in blue-tinted blotting paper for eating on the run.

Johan grabbed several maps and papers with figures, stuffing them into a folio. An illuminated volume also. These he handed to Ynghild, trading her for the food. He nodded towards the door, indicating he was ready, and they filed out.

"Council Chambers," Ynghild said to one of the guards, who nodded in response. He trodded down the long spiral staircase ahead of them. As they passed the floor below, a guard joined in front and behind them, bookending the short procession with a security detail.

Three floors below, Johan was just finishing the roll. As they entered the attic-space hall where the Council gathered, Johan leaned towards an attendant and mouthed the word "beer" while miming a cup raising to his lips. She smiled in recognition and ran off to help.

The rest of the council, made up of the richest and most powerful Ivonian families, were there and seated. Johan's father sat in the premier position for the C'Antrells, and they shared a respectful nod.

"Good afternoon," he said to the assembly, then turned to Ynghild, "what do we have on the docket today?"

"The usual miscellany, Ivon Nova. Trade figures most heavily on the minds of the Council, as evidenced by their requests for agenda items. Commerce is good, and many wish to find ways to expand our opportunities abroad."

The assembly erupted into a bluster of nods and approving sounds. Johan smiled. "We are of one mind!" he shouted, continuing in a more tempered tone, "Ivonia needs a larger audience for her plays. But tell me, gentlefolk, what are your ideas?"

Vincent Lamoureux du Canapé, a physically well-rounded young man with a short dark beard to match his short, dark hair, rose, his expression begging to be heard. Johan inclined his head, indicating Lamoureux had the floor.

"I think that we might consider consolidating the trade fleets of the Veyns and East Ivonsport into our own, centralizing trade under our leadership. Reduced competition will allow us to sell our goods at every port, at whatever price we set."

Joseif C'Antrell nearly leapt out of his chair to counter. "That is a very short-sighted strategy! Competition and a free market drive a healthy economy!"

"But not," Lamoureux countered, "the most profitable model for us, the owners of the fleets. We've carried this nation long enough under the failed model of a free market. It is time for us to get our fair share."

Johan watched with interest as his father, a life-long politician and successful businessman, sparred publicly with one of the richest men in Ivonia. *I'm happy to share the load,* he thought, *but what is Lamoureux getting at? He knows full well that our economy is flying. Is he just jockeying for position, taking the contrary point? He can't believe that the inevitable war following such an action would be good for anyone.*

"Failed Free Market, you say?" challenged the Ivon Nova. "How drole! Lamoureux, have you been suffering losses in the market I haven't heard about? Ynghild here was certain you've made a killing since the Ivon Prior's passing. Was she misled?"

"Of course not!" Lamoureux's frustration at this turn was palpable. "It is only through my great talent that my fleet continues to prosper. But I have heard many people say that other, very rich men are suffering. All because of this administration's failed policies!"

"Interesting," replied Johan calmly, "Ynghild, have you heard this news?"

"I have not, Ivon Nova," she said with a practiced curtsey.

"Hm," Johan said, pulling the conversational reins harder, "What does the council say? Are any of you amongst the traders that are so harmed by the free market?"

Johan looked up and down the table, making eye contact with each person. He finished his visual transit on Lamoureux, whose face had turned a bright red.

"Master du Canapé," Johan started, "the faces around us account for fully eighty percent of the wealth of this city. Who are you speaking with that has this experience? Which "very rich men" are "suffering" the effects of the free market, as you say?"

"Wealth is relative," Lamoureux whined, "and I would not design to embarrass them in such a public place. I will meet with them before revealing their concerns in this venerated company." The pudgy man sat back down and studied his tea.

"A reasonable choice," lauded Johan, "so I ask, are there other voices that wish to be heard on trade and the market?"

"I wish there were more options. More places to trade with. The Cyfandir is only so big." The woman at the back was Fenna, a powerfully built former sea captain who now boasted a large fleet. She spoke from a seated position. As always, her words were short, powerful and to the point.

"That," said Johan, wagging a finger, "is right where I was headed. We do need more places, and I think I've found one. Yng? Would you walk these around the room for me? Thank you." He handed her several maps, first one with two following. As he changed focus, she selected the most applicable map.

"We know that the Cyfandir, while it does provide everything we need, is a limited space with a limited climate. That to the east and west of us, there is nothing close enough to make sense for a trading voyage. To the north, ice. Endless ice. And to the south…" he nodded for Ynghild to show the next map, "The Winding[8]."

Every former sailor and captain in the room shifted uncomfortably, harrummphs and nervous gestures spreading from one to the next. Ynghild grinned. There was nothing she loved more than to watch strong men become uncomfortable.

"I know, it is a difficult subject."

"Uncomfortable is only the start!" objected Fenna. "The only way to cross the Winding is as a corpse. The Winding blows. Not worth it!"

"Except that it is worth it." Johan spoke now in a foreign tongue that none in the room recognized. "The Winding can be crossed, and I know the first steps to the secret. We will find the rest of the steps at the land once called Mirekka."

Slack-jawed faces and looks of confusion and concern painted everyone's face. Ynghild returned to the head of the table and placed a hand on Johan's shoulder. Her face showed outright consternation.

"This isn't the place for party tricks. Speak plainly to these people, or you will lose them."

"Show them the third map. That one." Johan was pointing to the map of Mirekka he'd located in the archives. He again spoke in the common tongue of the Cyfandir.

"That was the ancient language of Mirekka. Does anyone here know it?" Stunned faces showed that he was the only speaker. "I found it, along with history and this map, in the archives as I was researching the great Dragon Uvrede - the one that attacked us this summer."

"When did you find time to learn a whole language?" his father Joseif asked.

"I'm a quick study," he lied. *I can't tell them I learned whole languages in the Dreamvine, they'd never believe me. This is an improbable explanation, but vaguely possible. It will have to do.*

8 The Winding refers to the constant, stormy wind that churns and blows around the equator; a never-ending, impenetrable airy wall that no sailor dares approach, much less pass.

"I'm not even sure it is still used anywhere. But the land at least will be."

"This," he indicated on Ynghild's display, "is what Mirekka looks like. A tropical forest on the eastern tip that appears to have a small elven population. A dwarven holt of some importance in the western heights. And a large human population right in the middle, where the Mirekkans live."

"That map looks old. Very old, and it does not show the Winding." One of the elder members in the back, a slim, bookish man who had made his fortune financing other entrepreneurs' adventures, likely knew what he was seeing.

"It is a copy. Might even be a copy of a copy of a copy. If it is as old as the Dragon, this information might be ten thousand years out of date." Johan sighed.

"But," Ynghild spoke up, "if no one speaks the language anymore, why bother to know it?"

"Because it was knowable, and just as we don't speak Mirekkan, what if there are people there that don't speak Cyfandric? It was worth it for the possibility."

"Wait - are you saying that Dragon was ten thousand years old?' Joseif flung his arms in the air in disbelief.

"Oh, not at all," Johan replied flatly.

"I can't imagine," continued Joseif, "anything living that long."

"I think she was closer to seventeen thousand years old."

The room was silent. This conversation had strayed too far from the topic. Ynghild tried to get it back on track.

"What is the connection between the Dragon and Mirekka?"

"An excellent question," smiled Johan, "the Mirekkans had Dragons."

Chapter 22

Scouting for Retirement

"Wagon is loaded, Artemus," said Floin, "and I'm as ready as I'll ever be!"

Mountain King Artemus finished his note, signing it with a flourish.

"As am I. This seals the trip, and sets forth my succession should we not make it back!" Artemus smiled wickedly.

"Is there something you aren't telling me?" asked Floin with a nervous laugh.

"Oh, nothing you don't already know. The world is an unpredictable place, and we might run into someone who wants us dead more than we want to be alive. I can't imagine who that might be, of course. I've no subjects that have killed several thousand orcs from the lands we are about to cross, and it isn't like you have a similar dwarf for a son!"

As they left the gate, Artemus handed his note to a young Holtgart, asking him to ferry it to Kelly Siegebreaker, the Argentine Holt's military commander. The youth saluted before running up the steps at top speed.

"We'd better put some distance between us and the Holt," whispered Artemus under his breath.

"Why? Kelly knows what to do."

"Aye, Floin," the King whispered again, "I just didn't tell him I was leaving. That is what the note was for."

Floin drove the pony and cart slack-jawed for a few seconds before they both started laughing. A hundred yards out, and the first shouts could be heard from Kelly, who apparently had other plans.

When the two dwarves did not slow or turn, Kelly went to the spot on the wall that had been acoustically tuned for loudness, and let Artemus know what the problem really was.

"Wait, Artemus! Come back!" The resonance sounded like a complaining giant, Kelly's voice deepened unnaturally. "I have maneuvers scheduled, I can't afford to manage things, too!"

Floin and Artemus simply laughed louder. For a moment Kelly considered mounting the white bronco that wandered into the stables bareback to make chase (however slow that might be), but he let the elder pair make their retreat, considering Artemus' written promise to return.

They rolled along until midday, when they paused for a lunch and a stretch before heading east, north of the mountains. This was a land of steppes and scattered forests, many of which hid below the plateaus along a maze of deep river canyons.

They rolled peacefully along the base of one of these canyons, an old path from holt to holt. They saw no signs of the semi-nomadic orcs that called these places home, nor did they expect to. Orcs were adept at staying hidden until they decided you needed to leave this existence, especially in this place.

They found a peaceful copse of cottonwood to make their camp, and took the time to build a deep stone fire ring before starting their dinner preparations. Two lines cast into the river near a submerged log yielded quick results, and they feasted on perch and spit-roasted tubers they had packed.

Dwarves like to eat, and these two were both hungry and well-off. They had packed enough to travel for weeks, eating like kings, so they did. They enjoyed a peaceful evening, readying a couple of berths on top of their supplies in the wagon to sleep in. They were just about ready to turn in, well after dark, when they heard it.

"Laughter," Floin whispered to Artemus.

"I hear," came the answer, "I think that way. Look, is that a fire?"

The pair dressed for stealth and started off along the steep face of the canyon wall. What the King had thought was a fire was a reflection of a fire around the next bend. As they reached that bend, they crouched behind a sparse bush and observed.

Dozens of orcs, half young ones, played and danced around a fire. Several females worked around a large basket woven from several layers of reeds, one bringing water from the river while others prepared soup ingredients on large, flat stones. After adding the ingredients and water to the container, several large river rocks were taken from the fire and added in, until the water started to boil.

"It looks good," Floin noted. "I'll wager it has more flavor than our bachelor's supper."

"Aye. But their dinner tonight isn't what worries me," observed the King. "Note the people here. What do you see?"

"Children and adults. Some old ones. Nothing threatening, nothing special."

"What do you mean by 'nothing threatening?'"

"I don't see any big scary warriors." Floin remembered Angus' battle at the Aureate, where he and several older dwarves killed thousands of orcish warriors. "Ah."

"Yes. And when you look at their supplies, what is there?"

"Uh, several more baskets of tubers and seeds?"

"Yes, but is it enough? It looks like we have more food in our wagon."

"Huh."

"We should prepare." Artemus rose and crept back towards the dwarven camp. Floin followed.

Back at their little camp, they discussed the situation.

"It's too bad. They might have a rough winter," noted Floin.

"They will. But perhaps we can ease it a bit."

"I don't think we can approach them safely. They're orcs, after all."

"Floin, I've been to war with orcs. They are a very dangerous and unforgiving people. But that last bit, people, is the important part here." Artemus waited.

"My mind is still on the 'dangerous and unforgiving' part. My boy did some real damage to them, and I doubt they've forgiven yet."

"I see," said the King. "When do you think they might be ready to forgive? When might they start to be ready?"

"Ah," observed Floin, "I see. When we treat them like people, they might treat us like people. So, what do you have in mind?"

"Let's give them the wagon and our supplies. This stuff will go a long way to making the winter easier for their small group."

They sat up a while and discussed what they really needed for the journey, and traded watches until an hour before sunup. Then they took what they felt critical to their journey and loaded it onto the pony – bedrolls, four potatoes, a small sheaf of dried pork, and the keg – and led the pony across the shallow rocks to the far side of the river.

Then they built up the fire with some larger wood, and loaded green wood they knew would smoke heavily just as the sun came up. When they were certain the smoke was too visible to miss, they started eastward once again, with a lightened load and lightened hearts.

“Maybe,” pondered Floin, “we should have left a note.”

“We left everything for them to see. What good would a note do?”

“How will they know it isn’t a mistake? That we meant to help?”

“We’ve been at war with them recently. Why would they trust a note?”

“I suppose you are right.”

“Of course I’m right, that’s why I’m king!” Artemus laughed. “But seriously, those orcs are expert trackers. They know this land, and to whom that wagon belongs. They’ll see that we knew where they were overnight from our tracks, and piece it together. If they don’t, we’d better hope they don’t track us.”

A whoop sounded from the direction of the orcish camp, then another. Moments later, more from the place they left the wagon. Then silence.

The dwarves continued on towards the Aureate, hoping quietly that Artemus was right.

Chapter 23

Gift or Trap?

Tashi was a young orc, heavy with a child that would be born in the next couple of months. She had spotted the smoke first, not long after sunrise. Now she called for the others, having found the wagon. She sat in a hidden position until help arrived, scanning the area for other signs of the people who left this wagon and made so much smoke.

Pema arrived next, a middle-aged orc. She left her young in camp, coming to check the situation. She saw no sign of life.

"So much smoke. It has to be deliberate," Pema said.

"I think it is a trap," replied Tashi. "Nobody leaves so many supplies alone out here."

"It might well be," answered Pema, "but why? Without our warriors, we are no threat. We are here, in our own lands."

They sat in silence for an hour, until they were sure there were no evil dwarves or men lying in wait for them. Then they carefully read the land. Pema reported first.

"There was a horse here. A small one. They led it west to where the river rock starts here."

"I see. I make out at least two different sets of footprints. Small, but heavy."

They looked at each other and said at the same time, "Dwarves." Sneers crossed their faces. Both had lost their mates in the battle at the Aureate, driven there to fight by Zonka's revelation that all dwarves meant to extinguish the light of orcs from the Cyfandir.

"Maybe Black Zonka was right," suggested Tashi. "Maybe they do want to kill us all."

"Let's read the rest of the story before we look for traps. Look, some prints lead toward our camp. Let's follow."

A few minutes later, they found the vantage spot from which the dwarves had spied on them.

"See the blades of grass, broken but still green. And the moss where they knelt - covered in dew. They were here last night, before the dew."

"They would have seen we have no warriors. Why did they not attack?"

Satisfied at least that there would be no direct fighting this morning, they stood and walked into camp, where Pema spoke.

"Everyone, we have an opportunity. Bring the young ones." She waited for the group to assemble before continuing.

"We were watched last night." Gasps and concerned faces flashed through the three-dozen young and maternal orcs. "Yet they did not attack. Let us track our way to that smoke, and we will discuss what to do."

Pema pointed out the tracks, the plant life, and took opportunities at each step to point out the nuances she saw, teaching the young ones. How to identify the weight of an animal by the depth of the print, determine speed by the distance between strides. Then when they reached the cart, she showed how to track through the rocks at the side of the trail by studying trace amounts of water plants and slime that was disturbed.

"We are alone," Pema assured them. "Those that left this cart continued, two walkers and one horse. They took some gear with them but left a lot here. Why?"

A precocious child spoke up. "Because their cart was broken, and they could not take it?"

"A good thought. Let us investigate."

The cart was in pristine condition, showing little wear even on the rivets along the wheels. It held blankets and tarps and food.

"This cart is not broken. The supplies seem untouched. Why would they leave it?"

They looked again, and this time Tashi spoke up.

"It could be a trap. To draw us out and attack us away from camp."

"A possibility," agreed Pema. "How would we tell, children?"

"They would have attacked by now?" asked a little boy, maybe eight years old.

"I agree," said Pema, "and they have not attacked. Why not?"

"I don't think anyone else is here," the little girl, about ten, pointed at the dogs. "The dogs are interested in where they were, not where they are. The dogs would know."

"But wouldn't the dogs have known when the dwarves watched us last night?" asked Sonam, an older priestess who led their religious services. The children searched for an answer, which a gentle breeze offered.

"The wind! The wind blew our scents towards them. They were downwind of us, so the dogs never smelled them."

"Exactly," Sonam praised. "And the fact that they heard nothing means that these dwarves were not wearing a lot of armor. I do not think they were warriors, or if they were, they were not here to fight."

"Agreed," Pema nodded. "These were wealthy travelers, traversing our lands peacefully. They came upon our camp at night, saw our need, and offered help. They left the wagon here and set a smoky fire to ensure we would find it. As difficult as I find this to say, these dwarves are friendly."

Chapter 24

Payday

Kesh and her companions, Nid and Nau, watched for the third day. The crippled human moved with purpose despite his impairment. He had more supplies than he would need for the winter, by a long shot. His shelter, a stacked-stone expansion on an older structure, would house their whole tribe easily through the snows.

"I still say," said Nid, "that we should kill him and take the place over. He'd dress out to a full meal or two."

"I'm hungry, too," added Nau. "And bored. I don't understand why you want us to wait. He has no one to help him if we attack."

"I hear you, I do," answered Kesh. "But I see something in his movements. A grace behind the hobble. Possibly before his injury. I think this person is very deadly. I also sense he has a lot more to offer us alive. I'm going to go talk with him. Cover me."

She walked as quietly as she could to stand behind the worktable where Brin used a hammer and chisel to split a stone. She was ten feet away when he spoke.

"Took you long enough."

"What?" she stammered.

"I've been waiting for you to approach me for three days."

"You knew we were here the whole time?"

"Of course! Your breath and heartbeat aren't like anything in the forest."

Kesh was shocked. *If he can hear our breath and heartbeats fifty feet away, this is a truly special person! I need to know more!*

"I figure," the man continued, "that you need something. Something you thought might be better with me alive. I suspect that you have been watching me weighing alternatives. Do you want to bring your friends out?" He waved in the direction of Nid and Nau, indicating they could approach.

Kesh turned and shouted in orcish, "It's all right. I was right, he knew we were here all along. Let's try to make friends."

The other orcs stepped out into the open. Brin turned slowly to lock eyes with each, smiling wider each time. Kesh was last and merited the biggest smile. She barely noticed the scars on the left side of his face, or his slightly misshapen skull that never healed correctly after the fall.

"Call me Brin. You have found me in my country home, enjoying a little time alone. My, but you are stout fellows, and I have so many stones to lay. I wonder: would you be interested in employment?"

"Kesh," she said, patting her sternum. She repeated the motion with her friends. "Nid. Nau. What employment do you mean? And how will you pay?"

"Oh, nothing untoward," assured Brin, "Mostly I seek labor to help me with this project. I am building larger quarters to keep me warm through the winter. I have gold, and there might be other advantages and opportunities as time goes on. There is so much to do, I'm happy to trade for whatever duration you have in mind. This could be ongoing, as I have more folks arriving in the near future."

"We need to prepare for the winter ourselves. Very few trading partners out here, and there are more of us. I doubt you would want to hire us all."

"How many of you are there?"

"Less than before. But still a few more than a hundred in our enclave. You do not have the space."

"I see," said Brin, "Would you walk with me a moment? There is something you should witness." He turned his back on the newcomers, apparently not concerned with his physical safety at all. He hobbled up to his workshop-turned-home and entered, waving the three in. They followed.

He stepped to the back wall and opened a small door - obviously made for a smaller person. Light poured into the workshop from the door, and Brin disappeared into the light. Hesitating, Kesh stepped in behind him first.

When her eyes adjusted, she saw a series of stepped planting boxes, filled with a variety of plants and vegetables. Some species were familiar, and some very different. The planters branched off from a central stair that worked its way down the south-facing slope, ending out of sight hundreds of rows below.

Above all of this was a glass ceiling, cut into a trench that obscured the greenhouse from view from all but a select few angles. This kept the air warm and humid, an ideal environment for a productive garden.

"All of this is fed from a natural spring uphill. I think it was designed to feed a much larger number of people. As you can see, I'm only cultivating a fraction. If you have gardeners amongst you, this could be a portion of the work and the reward."

The orcs were flabbergasted. Usually, they moved from place to place to find the best environment for the season, but this might be the best environ for all seasons. Nid and Nau nodded at Kesh, who spoke again to Brin.

"We are definitely interested. We would need to build places to stay nearby."

"Not just nearby, I hope. Let us protect this with a settlement right outside. All I ask is that we keep this place the secret I know it to be. It is a large resource, but finite."

"We will go discuss with our kin and return with an answer. Thank you!" With that, the orcs rushed out and met with their people, who were camped in the valley below.

Chapter 25

Cordially Invited

"Yes, the tower set needs to appear here within a second or two while the crowd looks at the dragon over there. So, some sort of weighted cloth over quarter-hoops, I think." Johan walked down from the stage and up to Ynghild, who held a sheaf of blue papers. "Are these for me?"

"They are *from* you," she smiled, "your invitations. Indigo-dyed vellum, with your logo embossed in silver leaf. Enough room for you to address them, sign them, and add a personal note if you wish. The calligrapher did an excellent job, I'd say."

She set the papers down on a table and handed the Ivon one. He felt the thickness of the paper, ran his fingers across the embossing, and even smelled the paper to be sure it was pleasantly scented.

"Excellent work, Yng." the Ivon Nova smiled, "I'll work on these tonight, and in-between rehearsals. Now that we have a good count, I'd like you to gather a few of the Angels to act as top-notch couriers. Look at the map, and group several invitations for each as they make sense."

"On it." Yng was as fine a second as any leader could ask for. "Are you going to rest?"

"I think I'll have time, perhaps, after the big bash."

"That is in three months!"

"And your point?"

"Even the Ivon Nova is human. You need to eat, to rest, to sleep like a human."

"I'll get there. There is so much to do, and it has to be right, Yng. Now hand me that quill. Did you get the silver ink? Of course you did. These will be ready by midday tomorrow to send with the couriers. Please, let's get the friendly ones?"

Johan sat down to the table as Ynghild strode off. He tried not to watch, but the woman was good at what she did. Within seconds, he was scritching his own style of calligraphy, entering the names of every important or powerful person on the Cyfandir. Long into the night, he crossed off the last entry on the list he went over with Ynghild.

He looked where the sheaf had lain. One more page. The actors and builders and choreographers were all long gone, presumably re-running the show in their dreams. The whole city slept. Not even criminals were about at this hour. And yet here, at a table in his own theater, with guards posted in several places discreetly, the Ivon Nova felt anxious.

Johan fretted about the final missive. The last sheet was the extra he had asked for, knowing that Ynghild might leave off Alene's name from the list (which she had). There was no one on the globe that meant more to Johan, and her name was not on the list. He composed his message on scratch paper for an hour before he had all of the words he wanted to say condensed down to two powerful paragraphs.

He took another twenty minutes to carefully transcribe his letter, adding in meaning to the artistry of the calligraphy. He hoped that Alene would see what he was getting at.

----- -----

Two days later, Ynghild stepped off the Ivon's personal yacht into the marina at the west end of the Veyns. She was dressed in her best gown, flowing blue silks from head to toe. It was a masterwork of stitchery, worthy of a queen, like the one she was here to meet.

Every other invitation had been sent with the best spies in Ivonia, to ensure a safe delivery with the proper pomp and circumstance. Impressions mattered in matters of state, and the Ivon Nova had entrusted her to execute perfectly. He did not know that Ynghild was delivering this particular letter, but it would certainly leave a powerful impression.

Ynghild made her way by gondola to the grand plaza outside the palace, and stepped gracefully off. Blue silk and lace hems caressed the terrazzo mosaic map of the known trading world, retracing her journey from Ivonal to the City of Trade. She strode right up to the palace and demanded an audience. Her grand presence and unshakeable confidence got her inside the doors.

There, a groom halted her progress, gently insisting that all audiences had been held for the day. At the suggestion that Ynghild might have to wait overnight, the shapely woman flushed and shouted and stamped her feet, punctuating her message of importance.

"The Queen will see me now! I am here with a personal message from the Ivon Nova, and I will not be delayed!" Her eyes flashed whites at the groom, who stepped back as if he had been shoved.

Alene, who was only a few hundred feet away, heard Ynghild and stepped to the top of the grand staircase that dominated this space.

"Send her up. I will find the time for this woman." She kept her eyes on Ynghild as she stamped up the two-story stair, waiting with a soft smile. "What a lovely gown, Second. Would you call that azure? Cobalt, perhaps? Or are you simply feeling blue?"

"As you wish, your majesty. I hadn't even noticed," Ynghild lied, "I was so wrapped up in this errand."

"I'm sure you never gave it a *Second* thought." Alene turned her back and walked toward her large meeting table. "Come sit with me, and do stop with that 'majesty' business. We've fought and bled side by side. To you, I am simply Alene."

Ynghild followed, strategizing how best to manage this gown sitting at a table.

"I hope you'll call me Ynghild, then." She took a place somewhat opposite Alene, who had settled several seats in, along the narrow end of the ovoid surface.

"Done. Now tell me, Ynghild, what can I do for you?"

"This," she handed the sealed, blue-glass tube containing a letter to the Queen, "is from The Ivon Nova."

"Do tell! What secrets lie behind all this wax and ribbon?"

"A personal invite from Johan himself. He has crafted a lightplay to be run at the winter solstice. They are already building the sets and running rehearsals."

"But that is months away! Why send an invitation so early?"

"He wants to make sure everyone is there," answered Ynghild. "It is very important to him."

"I don't buy it. It is merely a light play. What is so special about it?"

"As far as he's told me, it is a celebration of all of the heroic deeds around the Dragon attack and the Battle of the North Green. He wants to get everyone on the same page with what happened, and how it happened."

"Huh." Alene caressed the tube, still sealed. "And you are delivering all of them personally? You have a lot to do, or so I hear."

"Not all of them."

"How many?"

"Just one."

The women studied each other, eyes transfixed as if they were dueling with sharpened rapiers.

"Then I suspect you know the full contents of this letter?" asked Alene.

"Only the basic invitation. He had a lot more to say to you."

"Hmm."

"You've had an effect on him, you know."

"I think you've had an effect yourself," responded Alene with a touch of irritation.

"Not for a long time," said Ynghild. "I've tried, but he won't respond. I want to think that it is his obsession with this light play, but I think it is something entirely different."

"It isn't because you aren't attractive. I felt the pull between you two."

"Alene, I am a professional. All men feel attracted to me. I've practiced being irresistible for years, on top of a modicum of physical gifts."

"More than a modicum," chuckled Alene wryly. "Your 'gifts' make you a real standout, but I see what you mean."

"I don't miss, Alene. I never do. Not until Johan after he met you." Ynghild took a long breath before finishing. "I think you've broken him."

Chapter 26

Abundance and Need

As the mountain that housed the Aureate Holt loomed ahead, Floin Thunderpick saw for the first time in person the scale of the collapse Angus had been a part of. He discussed this with Artemus as they led the laden pony together.

"Artemus, that is the single largest shifting of rock and soil I've ever seen. Yet I can see it stopped right where it needed to in order to keep the outer holtwall in place. How did it happen? Was it another accident?"

"It was no accident, friend," Artemus replied. "The old dwarves are very good and very bored. They've been working on that trap for hundreds of years. But let them tell you about it. Act surprised. That may have been their last battle."

"So where was Angus standing?"

Artemus paused and leaned in to point at a black stone outcropping right where a steam-powered gantry crane seemed to bring supplies. "There. That little black rock."

"It's barely bigger than a dwarf! And they set my boy at risk like that?"

Artemus laughed. "Aye. But harmless fun is fair play, is it not?"

"That's my boy we are talking about, Art."

"They didn't have a lot of choice."

The pair walked on for another half-hour before reaching the small trail that had been carved to reach the Holt. They were both grateful that they did not have to ascend the long, winding road that used to take the better part of an hour to climb. The contraption they approached made both uncomfortable.

"That's a lot of iron," noted Floin, "But I imagine it would take a small forest to use timber. What is that, fifteen hundred feet up?"

It was a noisy contrivance, too. Gears meshed and lines strained as a large platform, big enough to carry several heavy wagons, made its way towards them. It was thirty feet above the ground when Alguin peered over the edge and shouted a greeting.

"Welcome, youngsters! You walked all this way? That's a feat of feet to foray afoot!" He laughed at his own jibe as the platform settled into the matching recess, appearing to become one with the walkway where the travelers waited.

"We had a wagon, but it needed to be somewhere else," responded Artemus, speaking loudly the way one does with elders about. "I wonder if you've a place for us for a time, with perhaps a cold beer and warm sausage?"

"Oh, we'll do better than that, Artemus. Who've you brought with you today?"

"Meet Floin Thunderpick of the Argentine Holt!"

Alguin's eyes widened as he realized his guest's identity.

"Not Angus' father!" he shouted.

"The very same," replied Floin with a touch of pride. "You gents had quite an impact on him!"

"Come in, we've lots to discuss. I think this calls for a party!"

They ascended the mountain, with Floin asking several times to pause the trip to look at different strata in the mountain. He'd never seen so much recently exposed rock, and marveled at the eons worth of history as they rose.

When they reached the top, they found that the gates they had seen from below were an illusion, a series of horizontal slats that gave the impression of a massive wooden door. In reality they were a pattern of walkways or balconies that allowed an audience to enjoy an unparalleled view of the sunset, rows upon rows of great seats.

Inside, the evidence of goblin mechanization was impressive. The dwarven residents insisted that the stonework remain easily visible, so steam lines ran along the lower corners of the atrium. And the light! At this time of the afternoon it was bright and airy, showing thousands of years of stone fitting and masterworks of masonry.

"It isn't at all the way I remember it," observed Artemus. "This is fantastic! However, the strategist in me worries that you've made a very inviting place for dragons."

"We thought of that!" exclaimed Alguin, "I'll direct your attention to the machine at the eastern wall of the atrium."

The newcomers looked, and saw a contraption that matched the opening in size, with smaller openings arranged in horizontal lines facing west. The number of lines matched the number of balconies.

"It's a pepperbox," explained Coenor, who had just arrived. "The biggest ever made. A series of siege bows are connected to triggers at each tier of the balcony. If a section is breached, a large bolt will fill the space in moments."

Artemus emitted an audible 'woooow' as he took it all in. These dwarves, alone for hundreds of years in a slowly dying holt that threatened to become a tomb, were experiencing a new life made possible by embracing and integrating ways that were very foreign to them. The progress and change was palpable, but the positive effect was obvious.

"The Goblins are working out then?" he asked rhetorically.

"'Ere," piped in Drailin, "let's show ye the kitchen. Maybe that will lend some clarity. Or at least some libations!"

The kitchen tour revealed massive automation, pipes and chutes, levers and buttons lining one wall. Alguin stepped over to one such lever next to a stack of plates and an icon of a pig.

"Warm sausages, you said?" He pulled a lever, and something plopped into a hopper above. Steam whoosed into the chamber for thirty seconds, followed by a short, shrill whistle. The hopper tilted, releasing a piping-hot sausage down a series of chutes, landing on a ladder-like tray. Alguin handed a plate and a fork to Artemus.

"Take it - it's hot."

Artemus gingerly stabbed the sausage, which was perfectly cooked. Just a dribble of grease escaped the casing as he transferred it to his plate. "Would you like to try, Floin?" Alguin showed him where to pull, and the younger dwarf followed instructions properly.

It took some tuning," said Drailin, "to get these to exactly the right temperature, but these little beanheads did a great job, didn't they?"

"That's somewhat offensive," said a newcomer, a goblin who stepped right up to the sausage lever. "And now with this machine,

"I – for one – don't eat as many beans! I am Mikolaj, but the dwarves here call me Miko. I don't care who says all dwarves look alike, I can tell the difference. You two are new!"

Miko looked uncomfortably into Floin's eyes while he pulled the sausage lever, never breaking contact. Floin cleared his throat and answered.

"Floin Thunderpick. You may know of my son, Angus."

"And I am King Artemus of-"

"Angus!" Miko nearly dropped his sausage. "Angus Redbeard? Angus Trollbane? Angus Dragonslayer? Your son is a true friend to goblins! I am so excited to meet you, sir! Let's share a sausage together!"

Indeed, the whole company sat together for a raucous meal, filled with stories and laughter. Artemus told the story of Scicthyis' attack of the Argentine Holt, with a heavy emphasis on his plan and the preparations for it.

"To this day, I am certain the plan would have worked," Artemus concluded. "But Angus had a stroke – we'll call it a stroke of genius – and dropped that portcullis right at the perfect moment to down the dragon is one quick move."

"Can you imagine? To face a dragon – it must be an incredible moment. Then to defeat one! A feat never to be improved upon!" Drailin was obviously impressed.

"Ahem," cut in Floin, "He already did."

"No. How?"

"Another dragon attacked Ivonia. A much bigger and more powerful dragon. He killed her in single combat as well."

"Nay. Not in single combat. Weapons can't penetrate their armor."

"True," answered Artemus, "and that is why he jumped downward into her throat with a magical spear. He cut up the sacs that hold 'er flame-making goos, then slipped into her gullet, protected in her own stomach until her neck exploded."

"He had to be cut out by a regiment of dwarves from the Smaragdine Holt," continued Floin, "and then breathed back to life by a young Ivonian woman."

The conversation went back and forth for some time, trading amazing stories and probing questions. An hour later, Artemus took advantage of a long pause to ask a question of the Aureate dwarves and goblins.

"You seem to be doing so well. What do you still need?"

"Strong backs," said Alguin. "The goblin machines are great, but our current problem is having to devise rigging and leverage anytime we need to move something."

"I'd love to have a gardener to share the load with."

Artemus looked at Floin, who nodded in reply.

"We may have a solution for you."

"Go on."

"Floin and I ran into a group of people that seemed to be in need on the way here. We left them our wagon and some supplies, but I think they need more help before winter. Possibly shelter."

"Well, we have plenty of space here. Who are these people?"

"Orcs." Artemus offered, flatly.

"Orcs?" asked Alguin, shocked.

"Orcs!" agreed Floin with a smile.

"Orcs?" asked Coenor, "like the ones your son saved us from?"

"Well, yes," responded Floin, "and no. You met the warriors here, and destroyed, as I understand the count, about three thousand?"

"Aye. A good start." Drailin affirmed.

"I would have agreed with you," said Artemus, "except that the warriors were maybe half of the orcs in our region. We met some of the other half on our way here."

"The young." Floin added. "The old. The sick. The caretakers. They suffer the loss of those three thousand and the jobs they performed when they were not fighting. Hunters. Gatherers. Artisans. Orcish warriors come from all walks."

"This group," said Artemus, "appeared to have some strong backs and gardeners amongst them. And as you said, you do have plenty of space here, even with the goblins."

These deliberations continued for hours, involving even Miko and some of the security force that Bedwyn left behind. After long and sometimes tense discussion, the decision was made. They would offer help.

Chapter 27

Top-Level Communications

It was late afternoon in the Veyns, and a stealthy rogue used the long shadows to conceal their approach. No sense in exposing themselves or their ability to move quietly and secretly across the rooftops and patios unmarked.

The rogue spotted their quarry from several buildings away, a red-haired dwarf with no armor, a bottle in one hand and a small stein in the other. *This would be too easy*, thought the sneak. They made an adjustment to approach from the south, as the subject was looking northward. A quick scan revealed no security, no one even within sight. The time was right.

The rogue hopped the last gap in roofs to land silently behind the dwarf, slinking easily up to stand right behind him. They took one hand to each side of his neck and started to massage stiff trapezius muscles. The dwarf started in surprise, but settled in as he realized what was happening.

"Alene." said Angus. "You are getting better by the month. Are you sure you are in the right business? You'd make a fine assassin."

"Sneaking up on you is not as hard as you'd like to think it is, Angus," said the Queen. "It's a little early for a bottle like this, isn't it?" She took the container and read the label. "It's Veynsian brandy, at least."

"I'm out of the Argentine stuff. This'll have to do."

"What's the occasion?"

"Well," Angus sighed, "I'm kind of thinking about loss. Bedwyn. Indaria. Powerful forces, lost to us. Bedwyn we won't get back, and if we do see Indaria, she'll be different."

Alene refilled Angus' stein, then pulled up a chair next to him.

"We all have losses, friend. Beatrice has been with me since the beginning, and now she's retiring to a place where I won't be able to get her advice daily."

"Aye. That's how I feel about Bedwyn. I only knew him for a short time at the end of his life, but I feel like I got so much wisdom from him. I fear there was more to learn."

"I feel the same. Bedwyn's guidance was critical to our attack plans on the Ivon. Our losses were minimal compared to some of the Ivonian troops." She raised the bottle. "To Bedwyn, to Beatrice, and to trustworthy advisors."

"Hear, hear!" resounded Angus, and they both drank deeply. "S'not all we've lost, though."

"You mentioned Indaria. She gave up her life for you and Johan, to release you from that awful plant."

"She did, at that. Then the tree ran off into the woods, and I felt like I couldn't follow her if I wanted to, and now it is certainly too late."

"Did you love her?"

"A dwarf and an elf? Don't be ridiculous!"

"You didn't answer the question, Angus. Did you love her?"

"I didn't get enough time to find out. I admired her, to be sure. But love takes a very long time for dwarves."

"Did you love her?"

"I might have, given enough of a chance. Even so, it could never be."

"Like Johan and I."

"How is that?"

"Johan. I'm sure that I loved him. That I love him, even, but it can never be."

"Why not?"

"I'm Queen of the Veyns. He's the Ivon Nova. Ivonia has a long history of trying to take over the Veyns. If we married, he would become the de facto ruler of the Veyns, just by reason of the size of his kingdom."

"Hmm," responded Angus, "I suppose there is a parallel. To what might have been!" He raised and drained his glass, and Alene mirrored him.

Chapter 28

True Lies

"When I was a boy, I loved stories." The Ivon Nova spoke to hundreds of people in a small amphitheater. "I especially enjoyed the more far-fetched tales, with dragons and orcs and dwarves, and elves!"

His audience had grown, including leading academics, career actors, stand-up comedians, and even clowns. They laughed politely.

"I enjoyed them because I never expected to have these elements in my real life; they allowed an escape from reality. But now... Now reality is different. I have encountered all of these things, and more! They are no longer vague possibilities. Dragons exist. Orcs are more local than we'd like to think. Elves, dwarves... they are all real."

He walked to a table which held several books. "And it isn't like we didn't know. This book here? A treatise on elves and where they live. This one with the slate cover? A dwarven tome made for us many years ago. This one, a discussion of orcs and their green thumbs. This stuff is real, and we've been sitting on the knowledge for hundreds and in some cases, thousands of years."

Now Johan picked up a glass-bound book, with intricate chains of glass forming the spine. He walked this one to the front of the room, where he presented it.

"This one, however. This one tells us about dragons. Not in general, but about the reign of a specific very old and very powerful dragon. This story would have remained an entertaining diversion as long as we confidently believed it was fantasy. However, this particular dragon visited us, and changed our lives forever. She proved, once and for all, that at least some of the fantastic stories are true."

Johan walked back and forth as he spoke, making eye contact with different people as he made each point.

"Now that we know that, it is imperative that we find out what we don't know that we know. That is where you come in. You represent not only the Angels of lightplay fame, but our top professors and academics. Our children's storytellers. So many forms of entertainers and retailers of humor that I can't begin to describe you all.

"And this is your assignment: take the blank books that await just outside, and fill them. Fill them with all of the stories you know from your professions; the things that dance on the edge of plausible to the absolutely impossible. Our first step is to collect everything we can find, then we'll sort, then we'll start to process." He paused briefly to let this set before asking, "Are there any questions?"

"How will we know whether it is a story worth collecting?" asked the person with her hand up first.

"Is it a story? Every story – whether news, bedtime, or niche erotica – every story is worth collecting in this exercise." Johan selected the next questioner.

"How could we possibly keep track if everything is written down in different books in a catch-as-catch-can fashion?"

"Great question!" The Ivon Nova smiled. "Each page of each book is numbered, and each book has its own number. When we process the stories, we'll use those literary addresses to index each one for reference. Those indexes will sort by where a story occurred, what time period is assigned, what names were involved, et cetera. Those references will be kept in volumes of their own, where a person with a point of interest – like my recent interest in Mirekka -- can look to find everything we have on the subject."

"Why do you need so many people to do this?"

"Another great question! We aren't looking for a large number of stories. We are interested in *all* of the stories, and we want to get them in one place fast enough that we can truly study them. You, I hope, are those people.

"The Bard Corps have started this work in earnest, but we need help. We need people who excel in a library, we need people who can collect stories from grandmothers, we need people who can chat with sailors and listen to the saltiest sea captains. We need all of the stories, and the existing Bard Corps are not enough."

"What if," came the next question, "we find stories we don't like? Stories that we don't agree with? What if the subject material is against our ethics or religion?"

"A very worthy question," replied the Ivon Nova, who brought his tone down to the very serious. "I have learned so much from other cultures just in the last six months, since exposing myself to ways outside my comfort zone. That spear that Angus used to slay Uvrede, for instance. The Ivon Prior acquired it as an interesting object d'art, nothing more.

"I knew of its existence only because he showed it off to me along with other interesting weapons in his collection. Only in Angus' hands did it awaken and show its magical properties. His handling of something we didn't even know we had saved our city from almost certain doom.

"The story that you don't collect because it doesn't seem worthy or because it doesn't align with your principles may hold a key to one of the myriad mysteries in front of us. We must not censor these stories, must not change or update them, in order to solve the puzzle of the larger world.

"If you accept this duty, you must do it to the fullest. Incomplete or corrupted information is dangerous to our process. Get every story, and faithfully transcribe them."

The assembly applauded briefly, then broke up into a cacophonous gathering of people, a crowd filled with conversations dividing work, territories, and targets. The Bard Corps was established officially, now they had to become a real thing by fulfilling their charter.

Chapter 29

Bits of Luck

Clean, pure dew dripped from one leaf onto another, gathering and increasing with each step until a small rivulet ran from the leaves above into a large flower that opened perfectly to gather it in the center. Once concentrated this way and steeped, the vines underneath carried these flowers toward the elves as they sat in silence at the edge of the sacred pool of Sara-Tholah.

Each elf raised a hand without thinking, elegantly formed to accept the flower the vine presented. As soon as the weight of the tea lifted from the vine, the accelerated deadheading process popped each from its verdant mount.

The evening advanced with purpose, and the moon held its station above them. Their view was partially obscured by the great spreading valley oak, looking for all the world like it had spent the last five hundred years there, caressing the stone with that powerful, woody embrace.

Within the tree resided a vine that twisted from branch to branch throughout a majority of the oak's frame. Waxy, oval leaves interspersed with the knobby leaves of the tree, making it hard to identify. Except there was one telltale sign – the large peapod-like structure that rocked gently above.

"Will she survive?" Endaria lo Thenalah asked, devoid of any real concern.

"I believe so," answered his daughter Indaria. "She is very strong, and older than I thought possible for an orc."

"Yes, the waters of the pool have a lengthening effect for most. In truth, had she not been the one to steal a bath here – what – two thousand years ago? If it weren't for that, I would not entertain her presence."

"Nor would I, but I cannot forget that it was her intervention that ended my time with the vine – with Le'el – early. That must be worth something."

"Not early enough, I fear," responded her father, who placed a hand on top of hers. "But this is our reality now, and we must make the best of the situation. And now I must know. How did your mother's Musing Stones fare through your time in the vine?"

Indaria reached reflexively to the hollow between her breasts where she kept the Musings. They were, of course, not there.

"I can't tell you," she replied.

"Why not?" he asked.

"Because I don't have them," she said through tears. "I thought of the problem at the last second and set them aside where I hoped Angus or Bedwyn would find them. I feared they might become corrupted by the process."

"A fair assumption," nodded the elder elf. "And a fear I have for you as well. Elves who escape Le'el have always been changed. It is why we exiled him."

"Why didn't I know about this?" Tears quickly turned to outrage.

"You were never expected to encounter him."

"Encounter him? I called him out of hiding! I knew the stories of the healing properties of Dreamvines, and I knew a story alleging his presence in the area where I had friends who needed healing."

"I understand," he said in somber tones, "and I saw as much when I encountered Angus after his escape. He was changed. Marked with green in his ridiculous red beard, and with marks on his spirit. He also had a resonance that reminded me of your mother."

"He must have found my satchel then!" Her whirlwind tour of emotion made a quick stop at the intersection of Relief and Gratitude, before traveling on to Realization and Concern. "I remember how you treated him in the spring. What did you do to him?"

"Not much. We talked. We broke bread together. I asked him if you had given him anything. He denied it, but I felt her presence. I think that the next time I chat with Angus, there will be a reckoning."

"You can't hurt him. He saved my life."

"And you saved his, but he has your mother's Musings[9]. He has them and he hid them from me. You know how important they are. How powerful. How irreplaceable. All of that is wasted on a dwarf. Wasted."

They sat silently for a time, nursing the floral tea. The Speaker broke the silence, in tones of a proud father worried for the risk his daughter took.

"One other thing he told me about. What is all this about you killing a troll?"

9 Elven Musings are deeply personal protections, usually seeds or nuts imbued by a parent with advice and protective powers intended for their child. Powerful elven mages can convey moments in their existence, allowing their likewise powerful children to commune with a portion of the enchanter, and the enchanter to open certain doors for their offspring. Musings are never shared beyond the family and cannot be recreated or duplicated. For Indaria to share these with Angus is unthinkable, as his relatively non-magical self could not possibly connect with Indaria's mother, and the risk of loss is great with the adventurous life that Angus lives.

Chapter 30

Tearing Papers

Queen Alene sat alone in her study, studying numbers. So many numbers. Her plan to buy and stockpile goods was paying massive dividends, with many captains taking the offer of thirty percent below market rates in order to refill their holds with different cargo that was more profitable on the other end of their loops.

Much of that outgoing cargo was from the stocks Alene had purchased, which she often offered for fifteen to twenty-five percent off the market rate. The longshoremen that had processed goods for the Trade Temple were pleased, as they still had the work, just in a much more sane way.

A very few Veynsian citizens were unhappy, as their predatory practices that thrived under the Trade Temple were rendered moot. Alene had retained several of these to help determine what market rates were for each product. That ameliorated most concerns.

Finally, a handful of the very rich found themselves without a steady income stream, and no interest in the new way of doing business. Of those, a couple simply retired and disappeared. However, several took their free time and challenged Alene in her meetings almost daily.

Avoiding those confrontations always made Alene happy to have time in her study. Today, she compared the city's expenditures from the year with the top-line profit from her warehousing plan. She was overjoyed to realize that now, with two months left in the year, she could cover all expenses if all trade stopped today.

It was a tremendous feeling of freedom. She hummed happily as she scanned for the next item of business. What her eyes found first was not a financial document, but a brilliant blue vellum letter with silver leaf adornments. She reached for it, then pulled her hand back toward the work she should do.

This came with the sullen, pouty look she would have adopted anytime Beatrice was cross with her. She turned her head around one way, then the other. She was alone. Her pout turned into a mischievous smile, cocked up one side of her face. She grabbed the letter and held it to her heart for a moment.

She slid the paper up her neck to rest in front of her nose, where she breathed deeply with a smile on her face. Then opening it, she read it carefully, fingers tracing the parts she knew were in his hand. *I was so afraid it really was over,* she thought, *when I told him it wasn't the right time. But this…* She stood and held the open letter to her chest with her right hand, left outstretched as if grasped by a partner, then she danced a twirling, freeform ballroom type of dance, all fast movements and covering the whole floor of her study.

She slowed, returning gracefully to her chair. She sat and swiveled around once with her feet up. Then carefully, slowly, she folded it back up and returned it to the blue glass tube Johan's message was delivered in. This she set in the nook at the top of her large, roll-top desk. Her break over, the Queen returned to work, one line on her lips. Not from Johan, but from Ynghild's visit:

"I broke him."

Chapter 31

Holt Up!

King Thannon closed the meeting with his advisors and walked to his quarters. He stripped off the pompous garb that he'd taken to wearing in his official capacity as the leader of a holt. As he did so, he remembered his father's words, "Dress for the job you have, not the recreation you want later. Never let them forget who you are and why you are in your position!"

Bedwyn had been talking to the newly promoted Sergeant Thannon at the time, trying to impress on his son the importance of a little separation from a leader and their followers. Thannon took that advice to heart, and when things needed to be formal, he was truly formal. He hated every second of it.

Now he prepared for rounds, and he donned a much less dramatic outfit; one more suited for physical work or travel. Still clean and in excellent condition, each element selected from the finest options, but work clothes either way. He flopped his hood back in the casual way he preferred, his outer layer hanging just over his deltoid muscles but not his traps.

Thannon worked hard for those muscles, and he had no problem showing them off. Now he strode out to check on the different areas of interest he identified as his responsibility in the meeting. He started, obviously, in the kitchen, where he had a quick lunch and grabbed a sausage in a small bit of bread as road food, a stein of cold tea in the other hand.

This he enjoyed as he walked the mile to end up deep in the bowels of the holt, at the junction of tunnels where the underground road to Seljuk lay. Bedwyn had shared the secrets he'd learned from Ben and Angus with his son before he passed, and Thannon intended to ensure there would never be such a risk again.

To this end, he had ordered a massive vault door with angled locks to be installed. When he arrived, still rubbing residual sausage grease into his hands, he quizzed the foredwarf on the project's progress.

"That rail looks complete. How is it working?"

"Eh?" responded the foredwarf, looking over his shoulder, "Oh! Yes, your majesty! It does work, and well at that! Hey, boys! Let's give King Thannon a demonstration!"

The crew stopped work and cleared the track of tools and leftover luncheon. They then grabbed the vault 'door', a thirty-foot long stone plug with the first ten feet one solid chunk of granite, and rolled it into the tunnel, where it sealed itself seamlessly.

"Beautiful!" exclaimed the king. "How about the locks?"

"Those are coming, sir. Bars will interface here, here, and here behind. This one swings in from that recess. But the real magic..." The crew pulled the plug back into the holt. "Lies in bolts that will extend from these holes. They are activated from a hand crank on the holt side only. And see here..."

The foredwarf led the king inside the tunnel to find the mating holes. "These, sir, we have lined with steel. It is overkill. But not the edge of this recess."

Thannon touched the interior edge, finding a sharp line on one side. "Ow! What is that for?"

"This is exciting. You see, if the people on the other side of this door were to hit it very hard, these sharp ridges would deform the bolts and lock it into place, making a new tunnel the fastest way in. You wanted it to be secure. We can't make it more secure than that!"

King Thannon left that responsibility with a flurry of 'well dones' and 'keep up the good works', then left whistling a tune headed for the brewery, his most fun 'responsibility.'

The taskmaster here was known as the Caskmaster, and he was proud to show off the newest offerings. Thannon's taste of the Tufted Darkshroom Stout delivered a powerful dankness mixed with edges of peat and mine tailings[10]. The King approved with a smile and moved on.

---

10 Mine tailings add a dwarven grittiness to certain brews. When you hear that dwarven stout is a lot heartier and more earthy than the human equivalent, trust your ears.

Edin's Illuminated Mossflower[11] Ale was poured into a glass next, and taken with Thannon into the next room. True to its name, the drink glowed lightly anytime it was agitated. The taste was reminiscent of spring water flowing from a mountainside surrounded by ferns and skunk cabbage, with a musky aftertaste and plenty of natural carbonation.

"An old favorite," the King allowed, "and well-executed. Keep this one in the rotation!"

Finally came another new offering, a Gingered Turnip Shalgam. This was served also in a glass, shorter and wider than the first. The Caskmaster narrated as he dribbled a bit of the purple liquid into a line on the tasting bar, set the glass at one end of the line, and waited.

"First, we set a fuse and swirl slightly to encourage the fumes to reach the right ratio, then…" there was a PHOOMPF noise as he lit the fuse with a burning punk. "This was first presented to me four hundred years ago in Seljuk, when trade with the goblins was still good. Try some."

The Caskmaster put a plate over the drink to extinguish the fire, then gestured to the King. Thannon raised the glass, swirled it, held it to the light, took a light sniff, then downed it like a shot. The Caskmaster looked genuinely worried. The King turned red and gasped.

"I said try some, not all!"

"What is in that? Lantern fuel?"

"No, in fact all of the ingredients are healthy, even before fermentation."

"Enlighten me," the King coughed.

"We use purple carrots, turnip, bulgur, salt, water, garlic, and hot pepper, then we ferment it in retired brandy barrels for a few dozen years."

"Interesting. We'll have to try it again[12]."

The King smiled. The product was still top-notch. Thannon handed off the Caskmaster's order for fresh mine tailings.

---

11 Dwarven mossflowers are used across the world for light, as they only require a little moisture to glow. They also survive desiccation for generations, making them an excellent method of lighting seldom used-tunnels. Best not to ask what liquids might have been used on the mossflower in your drink, however. Dwarves are creative in a pinch.

12 He was lying, of course. While he appreciated the show, the after-effects were moving and fragrant.

“I’m looking forward to trying that Green-Gritted Guster. Let me know when it’s ready!”

Thannon continued on to admire the freshened defenses at the gate. The need for an update centered around the very public knowledge that Bedwyn no longer resided at the Smaragdine Holt, and some ne’er do well group might imagine an opportunity.

Whether this threat was real or imagined, Thannon was confident that there was less opportunity now than six months ago. The Holt was safe.

Chapter 32

Working Out

Brin watched with satisfaction as the garden thrived under the efforts of the orc gardeners. They had most of the planting boxes filled now, mostly with native tubers they had transplanted and other crops already in-progress. *This was a good choice,* he thought. He smiled at one of the orc children as they ran by.

He walked through the expanded door into what had been his workshop home, now a mere connecting room in the growing fortress. These orcs were not skilled builders, but they were fast learners. As soon as they had built several walls with Brin, they were able to replicate the process as well as a journeyman worker.

Now all Brin needed to do was draw out about a hundred linear feet of wall to be built that day, directly on the ground. He added notations showing where windows and doorways were. By evening, the walls were up and finished, without a single complaint. If these orcs didn't respect him, he was way off base.

The day after a room was finished, another team of orcs would bring materials and build a serviceable roof. In this way the building grew by the day, feeling like a race to beat the snow. Preparing for that, a final team gathered materials to be able to finish the insides of these walls, throw and fire pottery, and perform other wintery tasks.

Brin was pleased. Also, he wasn't sure what these folk would say when goblins arrived with his S.P.I.D.E.R. A risk, but one he would deal with when the time arrived. These were hard-working folk. None of the aggression that he'd been led to believe were de rigueur for orcs. He spent a lot of time thinking about this and observing them.

He started keeping notes. Notes in a code, of course, which might appear to a casual reader as someone keeping track of the movements of animals and growth patterns of plants. In actuality, they contained the names of all one hundred and twelve orcs that had come to live there.

These notes showed general attitudes, skills, strengths, and weaknesses. If an orc was missing an arm, that might affect productivity or which roles an individual was suited to. Perhaps most importantly was a measure of an individual's moral flexibility or rigidity. Notably absent? Gender or age notes.

Brin knew that the greatest treasure trove lay below them, a whole city of resources, silently guarded by the corpses of thousands of goblins. With years of effort and a lot of rigging, Brin could make a living salvaging the items within. With a half-dozen strong backs and the right minds? He could make a fortune in months.

Chapter 33

A Teapot's Whistle

"No, Lamoureux, tariffs are not the way." The Ivon Nova slapped the table at the council meeting. "Free trade is the law of the land, and I will not stand by while you undermine it."

"Law of the land?" Lamoreux de Canapes yelled with feigned outrage. "You make it sound as if our Council is nothing more than a group of powerless advisors. We hold the wealth of Ivonia. We hold the true power. Do I need to remind you how you got where you are, 'Ivon Nova'?"

Johan closed his eyes and counted to three before responding. He walked calmly over to the angry noble, the rest of the room silent. He dragged a chair as he approached Lamoreux, and kicked the foot of his chair sideways, swiveling the seated man to face him. He slammed down the new chair to face his foe, stepping over the back of the chair before sitting in it.

"Potentia per Sanguinem." Despite a blur and rustle of cloth occurring below their eyeline, Johan never broke eye contact. A beautiful knife lay at Lamoreux's jugular. "I used this knife. Would you care for a shot at the title?"

"He hasn't challenged you, Ivon Nova." Ynghild was at their side, protesting the fight. "I doubt Master de Canapes wishes to make such a challenge today. Is that correct?"

"I issue no challenge today." Lamoreux sneered.

"Then we are finished," Ynghild announced. "Gentles, we have had enough excitement for the day. Let us return to work tomorrow. Perhaps with a little more decorum?" She shot dirty looks at both men. The Ivon Nova rose and turned his back on Lamoreux before heading to his notes.

"I'll be at the Palace of Lights if anyone needs me. We have so much to rehearse, and so little time, especially if I am about to become an Ivon Prior." He did not turn to gather the response.

The Council disbanded with a harumphing murmur, heading in different directions for their respective homes. Lamoreux headed for a lounge with smoke and sofas and cocktails, paying for a private room, and paying extra for discretion. Hors d'oeuvres arrived along with several of his guests, a half-dozen other councilmen who had witnessed this afternoon's fireworks.

"Well, wasn't that fun?" asked Savat, a playboy with slicked-back hair and impeccable fashion. His wine sloshed right at the edge of spilling, but magically stayed contained in his goblet; complicated garnishes still balanced precipitously on the edge. Savat knew the game despite being only in his thirties. "I'm surprised that you didn't take him up on his offer, Lamb."

"It wasn't the right time," responded Lamoreux. "But when the right time comes, I'll be more than happy to oblige."

"Today was embarrassing," said Garell, a man late in life, but still in full control of his faculties. "You would not have advanced today, old boy. I'm not convinced you would advance without help. C'Antrell is a potent adversary."

"We have to do something," shot back Lamoreux. "Every time I – we – present a plan to expand our financial horizons, he shoots us down! One might think he likes the poor just as well as us!"

They all laughed at that one – the very rich often have a hard time relating to the struggles of the working class. It was simply unthinkable that a rich noble, now a monarch, would value an everyman who could not advance his interests as much as one who could turn the tables with a large purse.

"Like us or not, I think he has to go," said Lamoreux. "Garell is right; I am not going to win that fight unaided. That's why I asked you here. I think we'll all be a lot richer if we supplant him."

"How will that work, exactly?" said a cloud of smoke with a woman's voice behind it.

"Policies. Fiscal policies. Whatever we choose, it will benefit us." Lamoreux continued. "Like the tariffs I proposed earlier today. The costs will ultimately be borne by the consumer, and if they generate enough revenue to reduce taxes, we will manipulate those codes to ensure we get the lion's share of the benefit."

"We are helping people outside our borders too much." Savat said, as he admired his drink by holding it up to the light. "Did you see how much we are spending to rebuild the Greenway's silos? Scandalous!"

"Agreed," responded Lamoreux. "I think we are agreed that it is time for a change. This Free Trade Experiment has failed, and C'Antrell must pay the price. Now let us discuss the steps between here and there..."

----- -----

On the other side of town in the Palace of Lights, Johan stood at the precipice of the tower that looked over the edge. They had raised it up another hundred feet to allow for more hang time during Angus' attack on the dragon. He shuffled his feet to the edge of the battlement-shaped platform and looked down. The hoop that surrounded the concealed, inflatable bag to arrest his fall seemed like such a small target from here.

He dropped a bean-filled bag to check his trajectory, then followed it to the best of his ability. One second, two seconds, three – BAM! A universe worth of air rushed by his ears as he fell, interrupted by the rapid deceleration of the fall bag. His hands slapped down against the bag after his back, gaining friction burns from the sailcloth he'd specified. *Gloves. The player needs gloves.*

He climbed off the still-deflating bladder, out towards the crowd. "Did it work?" he asked anxiously.

"You are still moving, so I'd say it did," said Del, the grizzled roadie and veteran of more than a thousand stunt shows. He smiled in a carefree way.

"The wind effect, did that work?" asked Johan, with the anticipation of a twelve-year-old with a firework.

"Ah. Yes. That. Well, let's see..." He turned from right to left, observing with Johan. "You'll remember we lined up several rows of chairs on each side, to see how far the wind could push. It appears that all three rows are several feet back, most on their sides. I'd call that a success, yes?"

Johan was laughing as he picked up the chairs, setting them up a dozen feet back. "Yes, Mr. Preston. A true success. And now we know a key requirement when we cast Angus!" He laughed for twenty minutes, and again after the next practice fall.

Chapter 34

Overcompensation

Angus walked up to the shipyards with Beatrice that afternoon as the shadows grew longer. They had received a note letting them know that some testing was coming up soon, so they hiked out to enjoy the spectacle.

"Did I ever tell you," said the dwarf, "that I helped test a goblin flying machine?"

"You didn't," answered the middle-aged woman. "How did it go?"

"The launch part was a bit rough. I think they used rockets."

"You think?"

"Well, I wasn't supposed to be on the flight. I was attacking them, and they tried to escape."

"Wait, you were attacking them?"

"It was a long story, but yes."

"How did you end up in the flyer then?"

"They tried to run me down, but I became lodged in the passenger compartment, dressed into place with so much force I could not resist, and then we were flying."

"Amazing. How high did it go?"

"I really do not know. But I can tell you what the top side of a cloud looks like."

"How does the top side of a cloud look?"

"Very similar to the bottom, just with more sun."

"Incredible. Well, you are here, so the landing must have worked out all right."

"Hmm... About that."

"Gierman told me goblin machines were reliable!"

They made it to the dry dock, where the giant, metal-and-wood construct that was supposed to become Beatrice's home took up three berths. Three long, low hulls – 'pontoons', Gierman later told them – were spaced out underneath a low, square building that looked rather like a crate, clad in shiplap from end to end.

In the middle of the assembly a tell-tale, rhythmic puff of smoke escaped a tall, black-iron stack – this rose perhaps twenty feet above the roof of the flat structure. A mere ten feet up a small flying bridge was populated by a goblin named Sergei. Two other goblins ferried hunks of coal to the center from a load one of the yard cranes had dropped onto the outer edge, each hunk disappearing into the structure.

Sergei had a set of notes and was adjusting different knobs in the flying bridge, which sported no wheel. He spotted Beatrice, smiled, and nattered to his compatriots to hurry. Laurent walked confidently across the top of the combination roof and deck to confer with Sergei. After a few words, Laurent descended and made his way to Beatrice's side.

"It appears," he said, "that we are ready. I think we are safe here, in case anything goes wrong."

"You aren't inspiring much confidence, Laurent," she said. "What do you think might go wrong?"

Angus chortled, masking as if he had swallowed a fly. Laurent continued.

"Steam is a fickle wind." He replied. "We tested the mechanisms and know what levels the structure requires, but now we have added significant weight to each level. We have operated everything one level at a time manually, but this will be our first powered test since adding so much weight. Sergei is building a much bigger head of steam to make sure we have enough power to raise everything."

"So, more steam is like more wind?" she asked. "I don't understand. What do you think could go wrong?"

"Er," said the man, "we might not have enough power to raise the weight. Which would be embarrassing, but also costly if we need to upgrade the steamworks. So we are pushing it hard to be sure."

"Do you think that's a smart move?" Angus took a step back. "I've no desire to be in the way of a rogue steamship."

"Sergei tells me it is fine, and I have grown to trust him. Nothing has exploded yet!"

"What do you mean, 'yet'?" Beatrice goggled.

Just then a loud, multi-tone whistle sounded, and they saw Sergei waving a thumbs-up in their direction. The other goblins hopped down into the same hole they had sent the coal.

"Here we go!" Laurent was quite excited. "Let's see if we have enough power."

The first level started to rise up, quite a bit faster than their unladen test. Two seconds in, it shuddered into place, locks throwing automatically. A second later the next level clanged to a stop, followed a half-second later by the third. The last two levels hit faster than a reaction, and the flat building stood in pagoda-like magnificence.

Far above, Sergei flailed ten feet above the stack, obscured for a moment by the smoke before falling back to the now-much-higher flying bridge. He grabbed a lever in each hand as he landed hard, and steam shunted to the four paddlewheels at each corner. The wheels started spinning instantly, from static to rolling along in the air, to a whirring blur. All Sergei could do was hit an emergency release lever, redirecting the steam to a vent that exited out the back of the device.

It was a good plan, with one oversight. So much steam exited so quickly that the stacked cribbing underneath was unable to restrain the forward movement, and the machine tottered forward in slow motion. Sparks flew from each of the spinning paddlewheels, which emitted a tortured screeching as they imparted their momentum into the drydock deckboards.

Moving at a breakneck walking pace, the machine rolled slowly towards the ramp that led into the lagoon. Now at a jog, it was headed downhill. It was sprinting along with men throwing lines and chocks to no avail when it splashed into the sea. Sergei looked incredibly unhappy as he secured the valves again.

"It will be some time to build another head of steam, but we got more testing than we expected. It floats! Congratulations!" The goblin said with a wry smile.

Angus guffawed long and deeply. Beatrice, however, was not amused.

"That's my house!" She yelled, coloring the sky with language too strong for these pages.

Chapter 35

Odd Parlay

Wheels of twenty wagons creaked along the path between the Aureate Holt and the orc camp Floin and Artemus encountered a week back. They were accompanied by dwarves of the Aureate Holt, a few soldiers from the Smaragdine Holt, and several of the goblins that had taken jobs in exchange for shelter at the Aureate after the orcish attack last year.

"It is very strange," said Drailin, "to be bringing relief to the kin of those that attacked you. But at the same time, I think it is the right thing to do."

"Odd times indeed," put in Alguin. "But we have plenty, and more than a little need for these people's talents. I think it is time we bury the hatchet, and not just in each other's backs!"

"Stop here," instructed Artemus. "This is a good place. Out in the open. Plenty of places for them to watch us. Gents, let's gather dry wood for a fire, and wet wood for some smoke."

They made camp there on the round river rocks, nestled in a long, gentle bend in the river. It was a horrible defensive choice. Now they stacked up wood for a tall bonfire and set it ablaze. The fire was probably enough to gain the notice of the orcs who called this valley their home, but making it smoky would add certainty.

It didn't take long for the smoky fire to make the connection. Within twenty minutes, the dwarves had been located, marked, and watched.

Fifteen minutes after that, Alguin said with a stony expression, "They're here." He stretched a foot out in his semi-reclined position, indicating the direction he saw orcs.

Drailin, who was facing Alguin, replied. "They are in three places behind you, Alguin. Was I supposed to let you know?"

"That'd be a good idea, don't you think?"

"I was watchin' 'em."

"What're they doin' then?"

"Watchin' us."

Artemus chuckled and climbed on top of the wagon with the tallest buckboard, which he scaled. He waved one friendly hand and pointed in several places, turning in a circle. When he had completed his turn, he grabbed a fresh roll and a stein, making a show of eating and waved the hidden orcs in.

"Can you tell which group might have their leader?" Artemus asked.

"Prolly the one with the flag." Floin pointed to the pole that rose from one of the clumps of bushes, decorated with flowers and feathers and bones.

Artemus walked a few feet past the edge of the wagon-camp, shedding his belt and knife, his surcoat, and anything that might hide a weapon. He took several steps farther, holding his arms out wide as if inviting a hug.

Pema stepped out with the totem pole and walked ten paces from the bushes. She stabbed the end of the pole into the ground and looked proudly at the guests. She stayed that way for several minutes, unmoving past breathing. Every few seconds, another orc emerged from another bush, until the dwarves were clearly surrounded and outnumbered.

"Why are you here?" shouted Pema in the common tongue. "What do you want in these lands?"

"We want no thing," responded Artemus with a similar volume. "Except for peace with our neighbors."

"It is time," yelled Sonam without hesitation, "for peace."

"Why," added Tashi, "should we trust you? Was it not dwarves that slew our males? You killed my husband before he could meet his child!" She cradled her belly with tears in her eyes.

"It is true," replied Artemus, "that many orcs lay buried in the rockfall at the mouth of the Aureate holt. They did not parlay. We still don't know why they attacked."

Tashi flashed her angry eyes at the dwarves. "One of yours attacked Black Zonka! She let us know that you were here to kill us. So we gathered all of our warriors and attacked. My husband led the group from our enclave."

"We did attack the Aureate," Sonam added. "It was a pre-emptive strike to prevent a larger attack our holiest shaman warned us of."

"Your shaman was mistaken," pleaded Artemus. "You see representatives of all three holts that border your valley. None of us were going to attack."

"Black Zonka is very old," Pema offered to Tashi. "She may have been mistaken."

"How would we know?" Tashi was furious. "We can't lose any more of our people!"

Both groups stood silent and felt Tashi's pain. Hers would be a difficult road, as would her child's. She had a right to be angry. Floin stepped forward, mimicking Artemus' actions to show he was no threat.

"If I may," he started. "You might know that, despite the orcs attacking the Aureate with Zonka, there were no counter-attacks. No dwarf left their home to attack orcs this year. When Artemus and I came upon your camp, we were overwhelmed with grief for your families. We left our wagon with our supplies to help ease your winter."

Artemus nodded and gestured to the wagons behind them. "We thought that one wagon load of supplies might not be enough, so we brought more. All of this is for you."

Alguin walked towards Tashi. "And if that isn't enough, we came to offer you a warm place to stay. It looks to be a hard winter. You would not be the only guests – after a terrible accident at Seljuk, these goblins needed a place, and they have found one with us."

Drailin stood and turned to the goblins. "And we are better with them." He nodded and turned again to Sonam. "We still have plenty of space and supplies. Take these to help with what your warriors might have laid by for your people. And consider joining us, at least until Spring."

----- -----

A truce was reached, and the two groups broke bread together and ate well. The next morning, they parted, with the orcs leading the wagons away. As the dwarves moved East towards the Aureate, Sonam approached Alguin.

"Thank you for being a good neighbor. This is unexpected. We will consider your offer." The orc gave a hug to the dwarf, which he returned.

The dwarves had a very peaceful, very quiet walk back to the holt.

Chapter 36

A Tangled Web

Brin reclined and stretched in the steamy upper reaches of his greenhouse. In the few weeks since they'd arrived, the orcs transformed his workshop and its surprise greenhouse into a lush garden with active compost heaps. Whatever processes went on inside those heaps, he now knew they generated heat, and he loved it.

His bones ached in the cold. Physical challenges after his fall were compounded by extra pain in colder weather, and it appeared that colder weather would dominate the winter at this altitude. But with this heat, he was as limber as he was likely to ever be. A gentle touch on his shoulder caused him to open his eyes. Kesh stood above him, with an expression of mild concern and amusement.

"Brin, some people have brought a thing for you. A machine. Would you like me to send them away?"

"No!" Brin jumped up, forgetting that one leg didn't work well for a moment. He fell into Kesh's strong arms, and she helped him back to upright. "Thank you, I'll come talk to them. You didn't hurt anyone, did you?"

"No damage yet. Maybe emotional damage, but not much."

"Good."

Brin grabbed crutches and tripod-walked to the gate. His workshop had become a small fortress, complete with family compounds. Those ringed a central courtyard, covered for the winter with timber and peat. Residual heat from the greenhouse kept even this area much warmer than the ambient freezing ranges. Inside the gatehouse, several goblins stood around a greasy tarp that covered something.

"Yerp," said Bazow, obviously terrified. "Er, Sergei asked me to bring your Suspended Person In Distress Enablement Rig, and acclimate you to its usage."

"Excellent, let us see it!" Brin tried hard to contain his excitement, but failed.

"Are you sure?" Bazow replied, "Here? In front of…them?" he pantomimed hiding his finger as he pointed to Kesh and the other orcs.

"I am sure."

"I mean," Bazow stammered, "perhaps an unveiling of this magnitude deserves some ceremony. A little pomp. A proper audience." He tried to get Brin to see his distrust of the orcs through not-so-obtuse gesticulation and meaning-filled eye rolls.

"Anything you have to show me," clarified Brin, "you can show them. They may have to help me use it, after all."

"Are you quite certain–"

Brin reached out and pinched Bazow's lips together, tightly.

"I am quite certain. And if you make one more nuanced overture or mention your racism again, I will instruct Kesh and company to educate you in whatever way entertains them. Do we understand each other?" He let go of Bazow's lips and wiped his hands on his jacket.

Bazow appeared to glitch for a moment, unsure of how to proceed. Eventually he grabbed a corner of the tarp and retracted it to reveal the S.P.I.D.E.R., waving his arms toward it in a comical attempt to mimic a spokesmodel.

Brin ignored the goblin, reaching in to check the harness, pushing and pulling on legs, hoses and components as he orbited the machine. Once he started asking specific mechanical questions, Bazow recovered and gave an excellent accounting of the whole machine and how to use it.

Eventually Brin climbed in, a several minute task that required outside help. He pulled on the controls as Bazow had described, but nothing happened.

"Well of course nothing happened, we've got to hook it up to steam first, don't we? Where is the workshop? There was a steam plant there."

After some more yammering, Kesh brought six stout orcs to each lift a leg and carry Brin to the workshop where the steam supply waited. After an hour, when they had started the steam plant and built steam, Brin tried the controls again.

Progress was halting at first, but the six legs worked together in groups of three to move forward and back, with a differential steering to turn like a tank. After two hours, Brin was reasonably adept at basic maneuvering, as well as exhausted from working muscles that were well out of practice. Kesh carried Brin from the S.P.I.D.E.R. to his recliner in the greenhouse, and Bazow followed.

"I'm glad to see you use it so well," applauded the goblin. "Now if I can take payment, I'll be on my way…"

"Oh, Bazow, we aren't done yet." Brin spoke with closed eyes. "I'll need you to figure enough flexible line that I can go anywhere in the compound in the suit. After that, we discuss true mobility."

"You mean," Bazow nearly cried, "to keep me here? I was going home!"

"Oh, I wouldn't keep you here against your will, of course," said Brin as Bazow visibly relaxed." But if you want payment, you must deliver me a product that I can use. Without outside help. You and the other goblins can stay right here in the original workshop. That should prove comfortable, yes?"

"With these… orcs? They don't even know what chairs are, much less how to use them. You must be joking."

"Kesh," said Brin loudly, "have you thought about how you might educate Bazow here if he keeps running his mouth?"

"Oh, yes," she responded with a very toothy grin. "I have many tasty recipes – I mean lessons – for a goblin like Bazow."

"I'll get right to work." And to Bazow's credit, he did.

Chapter 37

Welcoming the Orcs

Tashi chafed at the idea of joining the dwarves, even just for a season. But for her baby, she made the awful decision to join Pema, Sonam, and the rest of the tribe as they headed for the Holt. She also chafed against the idea that these mules should be beasts of burden and not free. But for now, they enabled the tribe to move much of their chattel quickly.

"I don't want my child to learn about life in a tunnel," she said to Pema as they walked next to each other.

"I wouldn't either. We won't be prisoners. We can make foraging trips outside every day. I'm sure they don't eat well."

"That is obvious. Not one was trim. All dwarves I've seen have big bellies and move like it."

"Tashi, be careful. There is often more to people than meets the eye. Zonka took three thousand of our people to attack them, and none came back save Zonka. These dwarves now welcome us in. Perhaps we should not speak poorly of them."

"Eych. I'm still not convinced it isn't a trap."

"It isn't a trap. Tashi, if they wanted us to die, they would have let us suffer through the winter. Think things through. I understand your anger, but it is misplaced."

Towards the rear of the caravan, Sonam walked with the children, answering questions from her students.

"I heard dwarves eat orc children. Is that true?"

"No," chuckled Sonam, "not that I'm aware of. All the same, be on your best behavior, just to be safe."

"I heard they ride dragons into battle. Nobody has a chance!"

"What an amazing story! Have you considered being a storyteller? No, people don't ride dragons into battle, ever. I'm not even sure dragons are real."

"But the great stories have dragons! Are you saying the stories are made up?"

"Oh, I like that question! Here's my very definite and final answer: it depends. Some stories are very accurate, very real. In other stories, details might be changed, or added, or withheld, in order to make the story more compelling, or to get a particular point across. And, yes, some stories are entirely made up." She watched the children for reactions before continuing.

"Here is the best part, children: all of those things are OK. There is a place in life for all types of stories. Some are better than others. Personally, I prefer stories that lift people up, and show the best aspects of others. Stories that make us want to accentuate our best aspects."

"Sonam, many stories make dwarves sound like truly evil people. Are they true?" asked a teenager.

"Again, most are trying to make a point. Dwarves and orcs have fought against each other on and off for thousands of years. I don't know why it started. But we do have very different ways of living, different principles. That gave us a lot to argue about.

"But here we are, about to join with them, even if only for the winter. I'm baffled, too, but I think we are doing the right thing."

I desperately hope, she thought, *we are doing the right thing.*

Chapter 38

Layers of History

Indaria let the branch of the rosebush take her robe as she walked into the sacred pool of Sara-Tholah. She stole no blessings now, as the pool had been exhausted of its magical buildup earlier in the year. Now the mild magics were largely taken up by Le'el and the tree he inhabited.

She took her time to wade, chest deep, from one ruined stonework frieze to the next. Unfinished stories, too broken to decipher now, surrounded her. One ancient juniper curved its way through the cracks, becoming one with a poolside column. Indaria had never paid it any attention, but now she did.

This tree had been worked, either through centuries of judicious pruning or through the manipulative powers that a few elves like herself enjoyed. She studied it diligently. She even reached into the structure of the tree, finding the individual fibers that lent the trunk its distinctive shape. It was there that she found it.

A message, written in elvish script by whoever magically worked this wood, long, long ago. It curled back on itself in three dimensions. The message was certainly safe from prying eyes, only visible to a distinct few. She started in the middle of the script, working her way back to the beginning, massaging out each letter.

It took hours. Her fingers and toes were pruny, and she was more than a little cold. But she had a complete missive, which translated roughly to this:

My time is short. I am the last who remembers the persistent darkness that took us. I take this seedling now, located in the sacred pool, to remind those that come after about the truth, and where to find it. Le'el cannot be trusted. There is another, Beh'lai. She resides in the old part of the archives in Ivonal. I have protected her with several elves to watch over and maintain her place. Please watch over them.

Indaria caressed the tree physically now, adding in the little cues she could to help the tree thrive. She looked over her shoulder to see the spreading valley oak that held Le'el and Zonka. She shuddered, then walked out of the pool and into the waiting robe held up by roses.

The forest brought her the rest of her clothes as she walked, eventually dressed in something an elf might wear to battle. In a way, she was heading to battle: to get information from her father. She approached the green, tree-lined area where the Council met.

As if bidden, Endaria stepped into view. Dressed in an ethereal green tunic that ran to his shins with a loose brown vest that dropped to his knees, he presented at once a casual look and deep authority.

"Father, I learned a secret today. First, that Le'el is not to be trusted."

"As we discussed weeks ago."

"This was known far longer than that, and I suspect you knew before I was born."

"I did."

"Why does no one else remember?"

"An excellent question."

"Why do we not teach about it?"

"We felt there was nothing to gain. Le'el was gone from our community, and never returned until you brought him."

"And now you are pleased he is here?"

"Not at all."

"So why tolerate him?"

"At the moment, he holds Zonka. When that resolves, we can have a different conversation."

"I've also been led to believe that Dreamvines are incredibly scarce."

"They are."

"And that Le'el is the only one we know of on the Cyfandir."

"That is as we teach it, yes."

"Why do we teach that?"

"As you've observed, it is true."

"Ah. It is true, as far as I have observed. But what about Beh'lai?"

Endaria clapped for his daughter, a great smile on one side of his face.

"That name has been kept secret for thousands of years. How did you learn of it?"

"It was written in the fibers of a tree, crafted in such a way that the calligrapher had at least as much talent as you, father. Who could that have been?"

"Another name that has not been spoken for a very long time."

"Since the persistent darkness?"

"That is something I do not remember."

"Have you heard of it?"

"Only in echoes of generations past. A time that no longer bears any meaning for our people."

"The surest way to repeat history is to forget it."

"That is true, but we had nothing to do with the persistent darkness. We merely survived it."

"What else can you tell me?"

Endaria pondered this inquiry.

"I have no more I can tell you. Hearsay is not reality, it is only an echo. You need a first-person account. Le'el could tell you, but he has been mad for so long, you could not trust his word."

"Beh'lai it is, then."

"Before you seek anyone else, you must complete your work with Zonka." She nodded, and returned to her work; a grimly stoic look on her face.

She looked over her shoulder as her father passed silently into the woods before allowing the thought into her head. She didn't think he was able to read her thoughts, but it had always been difficult to keep anything from him. *I have to know. For my sanity. For their sake.*

She lifted her hands from her belly where they were fretting, and climbed up into the tree near Zonka's pod. Without making contact, she considered the ancient orc's plight.

"If I don't go, I can make this time easier for you, but my own will suffer. If I do go, I might lose you, the person I never expected as a friend and mentor; but what mine will gain, and what the world may gain… the potential gains are too much to ignore. I'm sorry, Zonka." *I'm sorry, father, but I must take the risk.*

Chapter 39

Things Go South

"After I completed my work with Zonka," expressed Sonam proudly, "I joined the enclave she assigned me to. It was only five years until Jana, my predecessor, passed, and I became the priestess. Fifteen years later, we are here, in the very heart of the place she convinced us evil was centered."

"Well," asked Artemus, "now that you've been here a few weeks, how do you find the home of evil?"

"I am shocked to say, but I find no evil. A lack of greenery and fresh air, but we can work on that."

"Sonam," said Artemus, holding her hand in both of his, "it has been a true privilege to meet you and learn about your customs. We are very different, but it is obvious that you want the best for your people, as I want the best for mine. I hope I get to meet this Zonka one day, to learn why she was so convinced there was evil here aiming to kill orcs."

"I think you both could learn a lot from each other, too. I will share this; she spoke of a red-bearded dwarf that came upon her at her home this spring, north of the place you call the Sliver. He terrified her and destroyed her homestead, with an army behind him."

Artemus and Floin looked at each other, then at the other dwarves nearby. An unheard conference ensued, arguments of the eyes closed only after Floin rose.

"The red-bearded dwarf is my son, Angus. He was taken prisoner in the forest north of the Sliver by elves, stripped and shamed. They found that his cause was noble, and gave him his gear back, sending him on his way. He told me he found a mossy place, like a knoll, and fell asleep right there in his armor, exhausted from his ordeal with the elves.

"A day later, he was attacked at the sliver by orcs, and he held a pinch point against the onslaught. Something must have happened in between that he did not tell me about."

"Indeed. Why would he keep quiet about such an interaction?" Artemus was likewise perplexed. "I can assure you that he was the only dwarf out and about in the area. There was no army."

Tashi walked in and spoke up next. "Is Angus an angry drunk?"

"Angus is neither angry nor a drunkard!" Floin tried to restrain his offense. Until the battle at the Sliver, Angus had only killed one being –a dragon– who was also attacking our holt. He was barely an adult."

"Tashi," interjected Sonam, "is also barely an adult. I hope you can forgive her rash words. She still mourns the loss of her mate, who died in the battle here at the Aureate."

"A battle," Artemus added, "that, perhaps, should never have happened. Where might we find Zonka now?"

"I do not know. I last saw her at a holy site in the mountains at the summer solstice. If I see her at the next solstice gathering, I will tell her you want to meet."

"I see. Where does this gathering take place?"

"Some secrets must remain secrets, friend," Sonam intoned. "This is one I will not share."

The dwarves spent the rest of the evening preparing for the morning's journey to the Argentine Holt. Alguin and Drailin, along with several of the Smaragdine guards, came along. There was a big fete at Ivonia's Palace of Lights soon, and they needed to arrive together.

In the morning they started a two-day trip back to the Argentine Holt, retracing the path Artemus and Floin had taken together. Snow and wind made it tough going, but the weather did not add much to the time. They made the Holt entrance just before nightfall, where Artemus set the dwarves to buzzing, getting ready for the next foray in the morning.

Kelly Siegebreaker cornered Artemus in his office. Frustrated about having to take up slack unasked, he laid out the law for Artemus.

"Artemus, we've known each other a long time! You know full well that I have many responsibilities here already. It isn't right that you expect me to cover for your absence and not even advise me that you are leaving!"

"It looks like everything was taken care of while I was away. Did anything get missed?"

"Of course not, I was on the job!"

"As I expected. If you want something done, give it to a busy person!"

"Balderdash! If you leave me in charge without discussing it with me first ever again, I'll quit."

"I understand totally. By the way, have I mentioned that I'm leaving tomorrow to attend a meeting set by the new Ivon? I hope you'll cover for me while I'm gone."

The verbal fireworks lasted for an hour or more, but in the end Kelly agreed. Artemus loaded a new wagon with not only road supplies, but dwarven finery, the kind appropriate for a King's meeting with the Ivon. He sent his tailor to Floin to make something special, as Floin would attend as well. It was, after all, Floin's son who had disrupted an attack by killing a dragon. Again.

In the morning, they made south for the forest road. Floin eagerly watched for the kind of magical movements he'd experienced with his son, but none came. Dwarven guards from three holts, all armed and armored, drew no attention – at least none that showed itself.

By the end of the day, they passed the southern end of the forest proper, and looked for the mossy knoll Angus had mentioned in his retellings. They saw nothing and made camp in the foothills.

They made good time the next day, reaching the Sliver with its open gate before noon. They checked into the Elvish Respite at Floin's recommendation, where they enjoyed a hearty lunch. A dark-haired young woman approached them, her hair styled to cover most of her face. A light frame showed, along with a light bump in her belly. She called herself 'Dar' and made conversation with the dwarves.

"Are you headed for the festival I've heard about in Ivonal?" she asked.

"Aye," responded Drailin, "but we've a week to get there. We're in no hurry."

"I wonder if I could catch a ride on one of your wagons? I can make a great salad for lunches in trade."

They agreed to take her, and she slunk off to her room to wait for the morning. In the meantime, the dwarves met with Noulish, the proprietor, near the stables. Floin, having discussed the idea with Artemus on their travels, revealed the secret of the door to the human, and they all walked in together to look upon the ancient meeting site.

A little water revived the glowing moss in small alcoves along the way. Artemus kept turning back because he felt like they were being followed, but nothing ever showed itself. An hour later, they emerged at the apex.

As the dwarven stone door opened, a frigid wind howled. Stone stools arranged in a semicircle were covered in snow and ice, and the dwarves turned back almost immediately.

"Let's come back in the spring," suggested Alguin, "my bones weren't built for this!"

Noulish vaulted out of the door, shouting excitedly. "A lifetime of waiting, and I finally see what it is!" He stopped short as his expression dropped to confusion. "What is it?"

"Come, youngster," said Drailin, "we'll enlighten ye back at the pub. This will all be here in a few months, but much more livable."

Chapter 40

Island Hoppers

"These change orders are killing me, Flannan." Beatrice's frustration came through clearly in her words. "I think we might finally be on the right path, but it isn't happening fast enough. And I feel like there is so little for me to do other than pick at details."

"I get that," Gierman chimed in. "...but I think I know what you need. Let's take you on the next trip to the atoll and get you in the sun for a bit. Remind you what the trouble is for."

"We can scout the location, plan the landing approach, maybe have a few days of fun." Flannan beamed. Flannan beamed a lot these last few months, a change from his dour poutiness of the summer. "I could use some sun myself. Heh, never thought I'd say that! The Veyns have changed us, Bea."

The three set up for a week at the atoll, which had a small group of stonecarvers readying marble blocks at all times. The trip aboard the *Aesig Picil* was peaceful, and they arrived at the quarry after only one night at sea. Gierman maneuvered the little ship into the caves, and they left it to be loaded.

They took the little rowboat out with a few supplies, aiming for an overnight at Beatrice's treehouse on the south side of the island. They studied the exposed strata as they transited, and Flannan remarked on his new idea.

"You know, Bea, I think I see a fault line that runs somewhat level to your beach from the quarry. We could put a tunnel in there to ease traffic, at least for dwarves."

"Oh, that sounds nice. I like the idea of good neighbors."

They found the beach that Bea used for trading with the Nyanjan and rowed right up to shore. After securing the launch and settling into the treehouse, they studied the approach. The barge would become a building most securely with a significant portion on stone, which they located at the upper part of the beach near the fish traps.

Flannan jumped when he saw his first troll, letting out a yelp.

"That's a troll!" he shouted.

"Aye," she laughed, "it is."

"It isn't attacking."

"Aye, it isn't."

"Why not? We aren't armed, it could easily kill and eat us."

"Apparently these trolls like the taste of seafood better. Still, I wouldn't ask one to dance – at least not for a long while."

"So you don't mind?"

"Why would I mind? I set up these fish traps more than a decade ago, making the trolls' lives here easier. Now they leave me alone, and scare off most intruders."

"Are you saying…" Gierman asked, setting Bea up.

"The best defense is a well-stocked pantry, yes." the older woman chuckled. "If women ruled the world, we would all be fat and happy. I tried to teach that to Alene, but she isn't convinced about the fat part. Give it time, she'll come around."

"I'm on the way to that reality," Gierman said with a guffaw. "If I keep on with this path, you won't recognize me in six months!"

They spent the evening lounging on the beach, watching the sunset and enjoying the tropical warmth. Bea introduced the dwarves to sea snails boiled in wine, which they picked straight out of the shell with bamboo utensils. After the initial shock, they found them delicious.

The next morning, they chatted and measured, measured and chatted, eventually delineating what they deemed the best placement for the building. Gierman took the plans out and waddled to the location of each of the pilings, driving a marking stake at each point and noting the conditions.

After one more relaxing evening, they paddled back around to pick up the *Picil* and head home for the Veyns. Bea was rested and restored, and the dwarves had gotten on with preparations of their own, which they did not elaborate on. Some secrets are meant to remain secrets.

Chapter 41

Greenway in White

Noulish saw the dwarven company off after a hearty breakfast, and they made good time on the switchback road down from the Sliver. Morning views opened up on this clear day, glinting icily all the way to the distant blue-tinged dot that showed the city of Ivonal.

In between lay two days' worth of journey across the best farmland on the Cyfandir –the Greenway. What they observed was not really green, but rather a winter wonderland already coated in a sheet of snow. The dwarves donned helmets to reduce the light in their eyes, slits properly sized to allow great battlefield vision while protecting against swipes and stabs. In this case they protected well against a glaring sun and the reflections that came up at them from the snowy ground.

Dar huddled under a blanket in the back of one of the wagons She hid from both glare and cold, and seemed to be out of her element. But she ate little and weighed less, and the dwarves didn't mind the company.

They pulled up to the town known as the Greenway as the sun got low and the shadows stretched long. After un-tacking their ponies and stowing wagons, the party entered The Hustled Bustle, expecting a quiet meal. What they got instead was a surprise.

"Trollbane!" rang out repeated shouts, directed at Floin. The dwarf blushed, accepted a stein that was shoved into his hand, and found himself dancing with one person after another as he became the reason for the party.

Mountain King Artemus and the rest of the dwarves found their way to a long table at the back and laid claim to it, watching as if the world had turned upside down. The people here really seemed to love the dwarf, a simple miner with a famous son. A large man came to the long table and selected a seat opposite Artemus.

“Your majesty,” he said, somehow both offering respect and teasing the king for being one-upped by his constituent. “I wasn’t expecting to find you here, but I’d like to take the opportunity to get properly acquainted.”

“I doubt I have a choice,” Artemus observed, still rattled over Floin’s reception. “Who are you again?”

“Call me Patrick,” the large man grinned his answer. “And you are Artemus, unless I miss my guess.”

“Aye,” answered the king, gesturing for the wait staff to bring a pitcher. “I heard tell of a Patrick, a smith at the Sliver, but this isn’t the Sliver.”

“True, when Angus first came through, the Sliver and the Greenway were merely rural hamlets in the shadow of Ivonia. But now? We are Gymdeithas Fasnach.”

“Ah, I’ve read a bit about you! How goes the great social experiment?”

“It’s grown a bit beyond an experiment, sir. We extend from the river to Canolbwynt Masnach, which you know as Veynsport. And I’m happy to say we have good relations with the cities of the Veyns and Ivonal. What I can’t say is that we have open and free trade with the Argentine and Aureate holts.”

“I knew there was a reason for us to come,” exclaimed Alguin. “We speak for the Aureate holt. And we’d be happy to set up a free trade agreement!” He pulled Drailin to look Patrick in the eye.

“Do ye have any need for gold?” asked the elder dwarf, starting a long discussion with the smith-turned-statesman. “If nay, can I interest you in a machine that spits out sausages steamed to perfection, on demand?”

“Oy!” shouted the woman behind the bar. “I’ll have one of those!”

Negotiations were long and amicable, and while the holts did not sign on to become part of Gymdeithas Fasnach, they agreed to honor nearly the same terms. By the end of the evening, all parties wore tired smiles and relaxed faces.

“This is how it should be,” closed Patrick. “But for now, I must bid you a good night. I have a long day’s travel back to the Sliver in the morning, then I get to turn right back around to see the lightplay the Ivon Nova is preparing!”

The large man walked up to the staircase, stepping over Floin, who had passed out at the bottom of the stairs. A large woman cradled his head and arms, stroking his beard with a sleepy smile herself. After hearing a snoring snort from the motionless dwarf, the man smiled and continued to bed.

The other dwarves followed suit, and in the morning they were all up and breaking fast with a large meal. They left early and retraced the different stories that had occurred in this relatively quiet place. As they passed, the dwarves were gratified to see that repairs were complete before winter, and observed a peaceful calm in almost everyone they encountered.

Chapter 42

A Stern Bowsprit

Bea didn't have enough time to properly switch from her island adventure to boarding Alene's yacht to journey to Ivonal. She brought her luggage straight from Gierman's boat and was only afforded one trip to grab a few things from the Hoot Owl.

"Hurry, Bea!" shouted Alene from the bridge. "The winds are begging us to launch!"

"I'm too old to run, girl. Go ahead and cast off if you like, but this is as fast as I go!"

A minute later, they dropped off Bea's things and made their way to the prow to watch the marina peel away like a banana as the yacht glided along, powered by a rare trailing wind.

Angus joined them with an armful of piping hot whitefish pies. He offered one to each woman. "The secret is in the fruity sauce," he advised, then shrugged when they refused. "Heh, I was hoping you'd say that." He dove in and said little more while he ate, leaning on one of the railings.

"I was hoping," said Bea, "to leave before winter. The portable tavern looks ready enough, but hasn't tested the same way twice. They say there are bugs in the machinery, but I haven't seen any. I'm told to be ready in the spring."

"Are we talking about spring already?" asked Alene sardonically. "I'm having a hard time getting through the winter."

"My dear, are you still pining?" chided the older woman. "I thought you had resolved to take some time to yourself."

"I had," responded Alene, "and I have. But we are headed to see him, and I'm sure we'll spend some time together. Heck, I'm slated to testify alongside Ynghild, about how Johan slew the Ivon Prior, and possibly even talk about Angus. It brings everything back up."

The women realized how public they were, and scanned the fo'c'sle for prying ears. Seeing only Angus near, Bea gave him a meaningful glare. The dwarf teasingly placed a pie over each ear and made a show of slinking off and out of sight. When he was gone, they continued.

"Well, girl," asked Bea, "what do you intend to do about it?"

"I'm not sure."

"You'd better become sure! Rulers who don't know their own next move don't last long!"

"That seems like good advice… but I still don't know."

"Do you want to talk it through?"

"I suppose."

"Let's start with the obvious. Why do you favor him?"

"I know it's silly, but his hair and his body," blushed Alene, "and he treats me like a demigod."

"Now you are just being silly."

"Maybe. But it is a part."

"He has always treated you well, I'll grant you that. I always worried you'd fall for a pompous jerk."

"I don't know why. You taught me to have standards. How do you make it work?"

"I'm sure I don't know what you mean." Beatrice did know, but she had never countenanced the fact.

"Yes, you do. You and Zidane can go for months without seeing each other, and when you are in the same place, it is as if no time has passed. I've never seen you with another, and he gives no sign that he is otherwise engaged. You are hundreds or thousands of miles apart more often than not! How do you make it work?"

"There is no 'it' to make work. Zidane and I are extremely compatible, and we never make more arrangements than when and where we might meet next. We've never discussed being exclusive, much less formalized our relationship. It just is, and we let it be so."

"That's not fair. So many people have to work at their relationships. It just happens for you and Zidane? Ugh."

"Every relationship is different, Alene. I had already outlived my first husband before I started caring for you. When I had time to think about whether I wanted another relationship and what was important to me, I was much more serious about it.

"I decided I did not want to spend my time feeling hurt. I did not want to pine. What I wanted was to feel joy and partnership, to have someone who I could trust to treat my spirit – and my body – with love and respect. I decided that I would be better off alone than in a difficult relationship, so I waited.

"And then I met Zidane. He was strong and agile, in his mind as much as his muscles. He knew how to make me smile, in every sense of the word. He is there when we agree to meet, and I have nothing but happy memories of our time in between our entanglements."

Alene frowned. "You are apart more than together. How can you know that he does not have another momentary partner somewhere far away?"

"Ah, that," the older woman offered, "that is the real secret, is it not? My husband never strayed, because we were always so close together. We ran a tavern together. I never had reason to fear his infidelity, because it was so obviously not a reality. But it was something on my mind, even so. My concerns for his activities were a source of doubt and worry, and needlessly so.

"Now my situation is different. My children are grown and far away. I have no care for what people think, save those important few in my circle. I don't have any reason to worry about what Zidane does when we are apart, so I decided not to. I made that decision long before we met."

Alene shook her head vigorously with a horrified rictus. "No, that doesn't work for me. If I am with someone, they are with me and no other. Ew. No."

"We are different people, Alene. In very different stages of life. We have different needs and different desires. You may find that you and Johan have a long and exclusive life together, eventually. You may not find yourself on my path, with a second lifestyle, very different from the first.

"...and that is all right. Your personal relationships are the most personal choices you will ever make. You set boundaries and foci that work for you, and find people who respect those boundaries and foci. If you are patient and diligent, you might even find people who enjoy the same things you do."

"Oh," Alene teased, "we definitely enjoy the same things, mind and body."

"Alene," tsked Beatrice, "you are all woman and yet still half-child. The conversations you have had with Johan so far – mind and body – are wonderfully compatible. But they are only the introductions to a much wider set of parameters that change and contort over the years.

"You've known him for – what – eight months? And in that time been together for a total of several weeks? You've scratched the surface, child. But there is so much more to learn."

"That's not fair," Alene pouted. "You aren't applying the same limits to Zidane."

"Of course I'm not applying the same limits! I've had my children. Raised my family. The only people that matter in my relationship with Zidane are Zidane and myself. We choose to limit what matters to us, because we can."

Chapter 43

Making Light Work of Lightwork

"I kill you for what you made me into!" shouted the actor dramatically, as he stabbed another actor - one that looked conspicuously like the Ivon Prior - in the throat. Red streamers popped out of the injured actor's neck, shooting over the crowd and settling slowly down onto the tables underneath.

"Cut!" Johan, the Ivon Nova, stepped to the balcony and watched where the streamers landed. "All right, this is getting better, but we still haven't covered the floor consistently. Let's reload, and add a little weight to the heaviest streamers. I want to treat everyone to a close-up view of the Ivon Prior's blood!"

He turned towards the south wall of the courtyard and shouted, "Over at the tower, is the dragon ready?"

"Uvrede is ready to fly!" came the yelled response.

"Angus, are you ready?" Johan hollered up at the top of the tower.

"Angus, ready to die!" this in the voice of a middle-aged woman. She stepped up to the battlement with a spear, setting it into a preset hole in the stone. Then she climbed up the shaft of the spear and leaned over it, pointing down at the dragon.

"Cue the Spear release!" Johan's loud instruction reached the right ears, and an inaudible click saw the Angus actor fall toward the gaping dragon's maw, all fierce expression and carefully aimed weapon. As she reached the dragon's teeth, the whole wireframe construct flew up and over the eastern wall of the rectangular theater. Air blew dozens of chairs over, and the actress was nowhere to be seen.

"Beautiful! We need you to be on the spear already, as soon as you see the light on the dragon. Great fall!"

"All right, let's run the Northgate battle next, places!"

Johan was in his element. Running blocking took as much time as running lines, just with so many more parties. He ran a tight ship, and since there were sixteen discrete 'stages' designated in this lightplay, he ran one stage to the next, with crews leapfrogging from one to another.

----- -----

The pressure was fantastic. Several stunts were literally death-defying, and he ran them over and over until he was satisfied – which he never was. It wasn't that Johan drove his people into the ground; there were always well-stocked carts with food and beverage for the players. He actually cared for the people he worked with.

However, his unbending commitment to perfection grated against the players and crew. Most seemed to accept his pedantry as the price for an excellent show. Some went home at night and cracked a bottle before bed. Only a very few held grudges.

It was these that Lamoureux sought out and tried hard to identify. There would only be a few capable and willing to help him, but he only needed a few capable people. A few very capable people. This was his third day lurking in the shadows, wearing the stained smock of a set painter.

Lamoureux also followed the plot, the sets, and the actors; especially those places and lines that Johan himself was to give. Just like the Ivon Nova, Lamoureux was a perfectionist at heart. He grabbed his brush and paint and repositioned to a new vantage; and continued watching. *It almost isn't fair,* he thought. *He'll never see it coming.*

----- -----

That prickly feeling was back, and Johan reached a hand to scratch the base of his skull absently. He knew the feeling well. It usually coincided with someone plotting how to kill him. He took the opportunity to look carefully from stage to stage, noting each person present. He smiled deeply, making a show of concentrating on how proud he was of each actor, each stagehand, each… painter.

That painter was hanging out in a place there was no painting to be done. With three hundred members of the company here, it was easy to get lost in the crowd. But Johan was a stickler for detail, and he made use of that knowledge now.

He gestured in Ystyr for his security chief, and winked at the painter who walked along quietly, two stories up. A quick look down to ensure that his man had indeed marked the target, and Johan returned to his work.

Fifty acting soldiers held back from the line of a hundred, each wearing a green sash; this left fifty in blue to be swallowed by those representing the people of Gymdeithas Fasnach. Battle cries and screams erupted, and Johan glanced up to where the painter had been. His man looked around intently, shrugging after having found no one.

"It is coming together! Now the heavy infantry and the fire…"

Chapter 44

Cold Welcome, Hot Meal

Ynghild stood at the prime spot at the docks, resplendent in yards of deep blue silk. She looked like a queen might, with a dozen porters and servants standing at attention in rows behind her. She held a smile that did not touch her eyes as the Veynsian royal yacht entered the harbor.

Ten minutes later, while deckhands secured the ship to the elaborately carved quay, the Ivonian strode to stand at the base of the gangway that would carry Queen Alene and her party. Alene stepped forward in a likewise grand burgundy gown, which achieved at once an understated dignity with several avant-garde flashes like a high slit up one leg.

Alene stopped at the top of the gangway, leaving that leg revealed as she paused to address Ynghild in her ceremonial duty.

"I answer the Ivon's call to attend the Winter Festival. I am Alene, Queen of the Veyns. Where is the Ivon Nova?" A fair question, as the Ivon would traditionally be present to welcome a head of state on an official visit.

"Welcome, Queen Alene. The Ivon Nova is regrettably deep in his preparations for the Lightplay, and he bade me welcome you on his behalf. Will you accompany me to your accommodations?" It was a lie, and she knew it. Ynghild had intentionally misread the timing to intercept the Queen, and advised Johan to be at the docks at sundown for a grand effect. *He has too much at stake to be distracted by a waif who fell into her position,* thought the woman in blue.

"I thank you, but I thought I might stay here with my ship."

"There is word of a storm tonight, I humbly ask that you come ashore and enjoy the lovely suites the Ivon Nova has set aside for you."

Alene thought about the offer before accepting it a dozen seconds later.

"We accept. I brought a dwarf, but he is sleeping in his quarters. Perhaps we can leave him in peace until he wakes naturally?" Alene stated as she slunk down the ramp. She smiled an entertained smile at the Second of Ivonia.

"Of course. I'm sure it is an honest nap." Her smile finally reached her eyes, and they walked together with a train of servants carrying luggage behind them. Ynghild stayed with Alene through the evening, ostensibly to keep her company while waiting for Johan – whom she knew would not arrive.

----- -----

Angus woke to find the sea calm and the sun setting. He quickly gathered his things and stepped off the abandoned boat, the sole sailor remaining offering a simple shrug at his enquiring look. So he stepped onto the ramp and descended to the quay. An athletic man approached.

"Where is she?" Johan asked Angus.

"I have no idea. I just awoke, and they were all gone."

"An odd hour for a nap, wouldn't you say?"

"I was escaping a little seasickness. It is good to see you, friend."

Johan, still dressed in work clothes from rehearsal, looked behind Angus at the sailor, who offered another clueless shrug.

"Well. That is a connection I'm sad to have missed. She must have arrived early. I'm glad to see her ship at least. Angus, my brother, are you hungry? I know a place right over there where we might enjoy a meal and a pint."

"More than a pint, I'd say. The beer was weak, but tolerable at our last meal there."

A few minutes later they sat in the barkeep's personal dining room, where they could stretch out away from prying ears. Closed doors and windows, along with a heavy dose of coin, allowed them an hour or two of reasonable privacy.

After giving their orders to the attendant, a familiar-looking young woman with a penchant for ruffles, they kicked their feet up and traded stories. Not their own stories, but stories nonetheless.

"Angus, I want to hear more about your changes." He removed his customary floppy Ivonian hat and pulled the green shock of hair out. "We need to figure out what is happening with the Dreamvine."

"Hrm." Angus took a big draught of his dark beer. "Well, it happens to me. I say 'happens', because it is not a soft change. I feel like I *am* the person whose memories or dreams I am experiencing."

"Like with the spear, right? You moved like an elf. More graceful than a human, and seriously more graceful than any dwarf I've ever marked."

"What are you saying, Johan? You don't like my dancing?"

"I'm saying I can't see how you could move like that, yet you did."

"Johan, for those moments, I thought I was an elf. A great warrior that had trained to slay dragons. And then, I was just Angus, falling into a dragon's mouth."

"And that is the important part. You slew that dragon."

"Through pure luck."

"That's what you said about the first one. People don't get lucky – at least not lucky like that – twice."

"Happened to me."

"Right. How many people have you ever heard of that killed a dragon?"

"A few, in the old stories. Artemus was there to see it happen for some."

"And how many of them slew more than one?"

Angus thought. He thought hard. "None that I know of."

"Once can be an accident. Two? That's a profession."

"You don't blame the Dreamvine?"

"Well, that's where it gets tricky. I think maybe. You said you felt like you were those people."

"Aye."

"I wonder, Angus, if we don't have parts of those people in us now. Maybe, effectively, we are more than we were."

The door opened, and a much nicer meal than they ordered was set before them, along with several pitchers of their preferred libations. The barkeep and the ruffled woman excused themselves again, and the pair ate for a while without talking. Eventually, Angus broke the silence.

"I touched a damned coin. A coin! And I was a money counter from eons past. Nearly fell off my wagon, all because of an old coin! If we are more than we were, there is less control. I don't like it."

"Interesting. I've never lost control entirely, I just add information. I can speak languages I've never learned, know stories I've never heard, sing songs that haven't been sung in memory. It is a dream come true for a bard."

"Schist. I sat on a stone at an old meeting site near the Sliver and I became a Gobleen. Got eaten by a dragon – yes, a third one. I touched another, and I became an elf. Touched a big spot, and became –" he shuddered as he remembered.

"No! Angus, were you a dragon?"

"Yes."

"What was it like?"

"Terrible. It was too much. Too different. I remember roaring, feeling so powerful, and then I passed out."

"Amazing. Where was this?"

"At the old council site, east of the Sliver."

"Wow. And who was in this council?"

"You aren't going to believe this."

"Try me, Angus. I think I know the answer already. It was everyone, wasn't it?"

"Yes..." Angus fluctuated between confused and concerned. "It was several groups of dwarves, humans, elves, goblins, and orcs! And... trolls. And yes, dragons. Unbelievable, isn't it?"

"No! It is totally believable! It fits perfectly with what I've been learning in the archives!"

"This stuff can't be written down. Everyone knows only humans and elves and dwarves can get along for any length of time."

"We do all know that, don't we? Except that it isn't true. We can work together. We can be better together. We've all been taught that diversity is a problem, and that different people have different values and should stay in different places. But it isn't true!

"Our diverse talents show us that if we work together, we can make *better* things, build *better* buildings, grow *better* food. And as I've been looking at the old stories, reliving some of them, the art, Angus. Oh, the art, the performances. Philosophy. Religion. Everything is better when we work together!"

"So how could that all break down?" Angus was confused.

"Breaking is the right word. Something broke, and the world went into a long winter. The sun was blotted out for years. Most people died. And the survivors seem to have clustered together. I haven't figured it all out, but life was better something like ten millennia ago."

Chapter 45

The Hidden Queen Returns

Garret Armand steered the ship he captained into the Ivonian harbor. He'd discussed this move at great length with the crew, since it was expressly against the wishes of the ship's owner. But circumstances had changed, and this was the place the owner called home now.

A rowboat carried a pilot to the *Hidden Queen* and the Captain ordered a rope ladder deployed so the pilot could board. A small bribe found them a spot out of the way, with reasonably convenient access to both the shore and the sea, should a hasty exit be required.

Once docked, Armand sent a runner with a note to the Ivon's Tower, then he waited. And waited. And waited. While he waited, he walked the market with his crew, buying Ivonian comfort foodstuffs to replenish the larder. Four hours later, he saw a group of armed guards escorting a man in blue to the docks.

"All hail the Ivon Nova!" shouted Armand to the crew, who echoed, "Hail the Ivon Nova!"

Four of the men boarded the Queen and looked for obvious traps, then stood guard as the Ivon Nova boarded the small trading ship he had once chartered as a spy. He walked around, sampling the goods, making a big show of the ceremonial inspection. Eventually he directed Captain Armand to join him in the dining room. They disappeared into the windowless space, while the guards and crew remained on deck.

"Armand, you've done well! How was the journey?"

"Well, Ivon Nova–"

"None of that. Johan will do here."

"Well, Johan," Armand smiled, "ours was a most educational trip. We circled the Cyfandir, and these are the updated charts. I'm keeping the originals; these are unmarked copies for you."

"Very interesting. What did you find?"

"We found a world that is much different than we expected. Human communities like ours. A floating goblin city. And a walled, modern town run entirely by orcs!" He pointed to the different locations on the map as they discussed. "This area in the north is only passable in the summer. We were nearly frozen in several months ago, but the *Queen* got us through."

"She's a good ship. I saw some samples. What did you bring?"

"So much. Some rare foodstuffs. Raw silk. Artful drums and some very nice weapons. But most importantly, I found a source for gormoital."

"Gormoital?"

"You'd call it mithril, but apparently the old name is gormoital, or blue-steel. The goblins at that floating city are overflowing with it. Do you know what they wanted in return? Grease! I told them I'd bring more next time."

"Fascinating. Did you hear anything about a place called Mirekka?"

"Not yet, but we weren't asking."

"You are now. It should be to the southwest, but I don't have easy directions."

"Not past the Winding, I hope."

"I'm not sure. But that is what I'd like to ask of you next. So here is what I propose. I'll buy the whole cargo myself, at fair market value. Let's move it at night, so word doesn't get out about the gormoital.

"With that money, fill the hold with whatever grease these goblins want, and make that trade while the invitation is fresh. Find out if they want a recurring shipment. And ask about Mirekka. Say you heard a legend about a strange land with wonderful fruit. Bring back any information you can."

"Can do, Johan."

"I'll send an invite for you and the crew to the Lightplay. You might take a few days to enjoy the port, and the play will be something to behold. It honors our friend, Angus, among others."

"Thank you! We'll be there!"

"Oh, and Armand? Well done."

Chapter 46

Chasing Stories

Ynghild stepped forward to the top of the Northgate Tower as the dwarven guests approached. The light of the setting sun illuminated her with a noble grandeur that she could hardly have planned. She called out a greeting in that formal voice she'd perfected.

"Welcome, Mountain King Artemus and retinue. The Ivon Nova rented an entire tavern and rooms for you and yours to enjoy. After you settle in, you are invited to tour the Palace of Lights, the Royal Gardens, and the Great Library of Ivonal. Come, let me show you the way!"

"We thank the good lady–" Artemus began, cutting off when the woman disappeared. Merely three seconds later she emerged from a side door in the gatehouse, gesturing grandly.

"You may call me Ynghild, your majesty. I am the Ivon Nova's Second, and I stand in for him tonight as he finishes preparations. I trust your journey was pleasant?"

"Indeed it was! I am gratified to see that the Greenway has not only been repaired, but seems to prosper! The Sliver's defenses are sound, and her people happy. And Endaria's elves let us pass unmolested. It was a truly good journey."

"Excellent," Ynghild walked quickly as they talked, expertly navigating cobblestones that occasionally conspired to trip a dwarf. "I expected a party of dwarves, I see one more that I do not recognize."

"Oh, that is Dar, a young person from the Sliver that wanted to see Ivonal. I hope you don't mind that we let her tag along. She seems to have a lot of knowledge for one so young."

"Does she?" Ynghild said with interest. "I hope to learn more about you, young Dar."

They reached the tavern and were introduced to the innkeeper, a short, beardless man with a middle-aged paunch. He led them to rooms, many built closer to dwarven heights. It was an old building, much of it stone. Dar was given the tallest room at the end, and the innkeeper ensured that the sheets would be long enough for her tall frame.

They met downstairs for a simple but delicious meal, and were met again by Ynghild and another group of people outside. They exchanged pleasantries with King Thannon and several dwarves from the Smaragdine holt, Patrick Smith and several humans from the trade cooperative Gymdeithas Fasnach, and Queen Alene with some of her retinue.

The Second gathered their attention once out on the street, waiting for two dozen faces to fixate on her.

"Thank you for coming out so late. Normally tours like these are held in the light, but we have some unique opportunities this evening. We start at the Palace of Lights, the very theater that we will see tomorrow for the Ivon Nova's Light Play. Since we are very near the art district, the walk is brief.

"You can see why we call it the Palace of Lights much more easily after dark. The designers and architects worked for generations together, finding ways to cast light at every angle. The result is this multi-story facade that dominates the space in the daylight, but becomes an absolute beacon at night!"

"How many people," asked Patrick, "does it take to light all of these each night?"

"One." Ynghild made an exaggerated gesture with her index finger, using her whole arm.

"Just one? There must be three hundred lights here!"

"Yes, just one. Watch for a moment, starting at the top. You should begin to see… Yes! See there, the highest light was extinguished? Watch the others.

Over the course of a few minutes, the lights extinguished themselves one after the next, from the highest to the lowest. When the facade was dark, the Second spoke again.

"One person just extinguished all of those lights. And now," she said, with a different exaggerated gesture, "That same person will light them all as you watch. A powerful smell of lamp oil wafted across them before that top light relit. Light seemed to cascade down the facade from one lamp to the next like a liquid, or a waterfall.

"Well, I'm impressed," guffawed Patrick. "I don't have any idea how you do it, but it is very attractive."

They entered the Palace of Lights and walked along the colonnade that Angus found so remarkable on his first visit, and into the main courtyard. Props sat everywhere, mostly obscured by tarps. One old man swept debris and streamers from the floor in measured, paced strokes.

"Tomorrow this whole area will be bustling with activity. It will be a night to remember!" Ynghild smiled broadly through the words, and led them through the back entrance to the hall.

The air felt slightly steamy as they entered a dark hall with minimal lighting. The roof stood fifty or more feet above their heads, stars above just slightly shimmering as they walked along under the glass ceiling. But what really stood out were the plants.

Trees from warmer climates. Bushes and vines and flowers – flowers in midwinter! – decorated every inch of these gardens. Ynghild paused, confident that the dwarves and humans would need a moment to adjust to the verdant reality that defied the season outside. Most people never saw a greenhouse at all, yet this relic was kept alive, regardless of who sat as Ivon, or what they felt about green things. The uniqueness made it a very valuable commodity.

Dar did not pause with the rest of the group. She walked forward into the greenery, caressing leaves and petals as she walked by. It was such a graceful movement, an observer might think the plant life was caressing her instead. She didn't pause, but took in every bit of the place. Indeed, her reaction became part of the spectacle.

"Very few people get to enjoy the Gardens," Ynghild explained, "But the Ivon Nova loves and respects you all, and asked me to share this with you as a special recognition of his gratitude for your contributions."

"I've visited Ivonal dozens of times, as a King," said a slack-jawed Artemus, "and I had no idea this existed."

"Aye, youngster," Drailin added, "This was not on my Gib On card[13] for tonight. I had no idea anything like this existed anywhere!"

"It is beautiful." Alene's comment was short and to the point. "I wonder why we haven't seen Johan yet? The Ivon Nova?"

"An excellent point, your majesty," replied Ynghild. "Perhaps we will find him in the Library. He has spent a significant amount of time there recently, researching old stories."

They traversed the gardens to another set of grand, four-story doors that led to a small, private courtyard, and into a matching set on the other side. Ynghild explained.

"The courtyard is designed to remove the excessive moisture of the greenhouse before it enters the library, where it might cause problems. Now, this door is noisy, as it has seen little use for generations…"

Indeed the door she opened creaked heavily and shuddered a couple of times. The air inside was a distinct mix of paper, ink, and age. The Stacks, large, double-sided bookshelves, were arranged in a semi-circular pattern around a central atrium. Each face had a rolling ladder to facilitate access to the higher books, higher even than the doors.

"It's a good design," Artemus said. "The sills are high, and the stonework is perfectly matched. I'll bet it is waterproof from all sides. Those stone arches are dwarven in form as well – but old. Drailin, do you know about this?"

"Not me personally. Granfer said he had done some stonework in Ivonal, long before my time. I figured it was long gone, the way humans change things."

"Not all things are changed. And some things many Ivons have protected for themselves. The Ivon Nova is passionate about these stories, this information. You are all invited to access this library anytime you wish. He would encourage it."

"But where is he?" Alene tapped her foot. "You said in the archives, perhaps?"

---

13 Gib On is an old dwarven drinking game where tall tales are written on a board with corresponding numbers, and randomly assigned numbered cards are distributed to the players. They take turns telling stories and challenging which of the stories are true, and with each story, that number is filled in on the card until someone gets a line connecting across. At that point, they must tell an entirely new story, or the game starts over. Each story is traditionally toasted, and as the evening progresses, players begin to match that toasted state.

"I did say that. Here, let me show you where it is."

Ynghild led the party towards the opposite end of the building. Dar spent a moment touching each of the giant doors, eyes closed, then ran on to join them. They descended a large staircase, finding dozens of people researching and scribbling notes in journals. None of them were Johan.

"It appears we have missed the Ivon Nova, my apologies."

"He was here a half an hour ago," suggested one of the academics, looking up from his notes. "He said he was looking for someone."

Alene and Ynghild both turned red, and Alene stormed out with her retinue. The dwarves were all walking towards a dramatically fluted stone wall.

"It's an old door, isn't it?" Thannon asked Artemus. "I think so. Drailin, might this have been your grandfer's work?"

"Might have been his early work, but this is old. Very old. I suspect it predates him, and that was… roughly eight thousand years back?"

Dar, meanwhile, found a bookshelf built into the wall next to the supposed door. She traced the tree-and-vine themed carvings, almost like she was reading in braille. They all stayed for hours, looking and studying the space, a space that was older than any of them had knowledge of.

Chapter 47

Out for a Run

Back at the apartments she had been assigned, Alene paced. Back and forth, round the room; she had no more patience. She found flowers and a note when she arrived, signed by Johan. It read:

My Dear Alene,

I rushed to meet you at the docks when I heard of your arrival. When I learned of your accommodations, I ran here, but was advised you were on a tour. I now run around the city trying to intercept you. If we do not meet tonight, it will have to be after the light play. Thousands of people depend on my leadership for that.

I hope to see you yet tonight, but failing that, enjoy the light play and I will find you tomorrow.

All my best for you alone,

Johan

It would be hard to describe Alene's frustration as anything less than a volcano about to burst. She'd traveled here early to have extra time, and was thwarted at every turn. *Is Ynghild trying to keep us apart?* She thought angrily. *Probably,* she decided.

The queen set her head outside into the common room of the apartments she had been afforded, and addressed her guards and retinue.

"I'm tired, I'll be turning the lights down and going to sleep. Please wake me two hours after sunup."

She grabbed two cookies and a glass of milk and retired. Ostensibly. Instead, she enjoyed her snack, turned down the lights, and put on the black clothes she used for exercising. With the lights out, she opened the tall window that housed a narrow balcony and plotted her route.

It was a reasonably secure location, too far to simply jump to the nearest step down. She was five floors up and twenty feet from the next balcony. She looked up at the blue-tiled eave above her. It would be too steep to traverse safely. The lead-lined copper gutter might be a better route. She decided to risk it.

She started by standing on the railing but was still not tall enough to reach the gutter. So, she took a deep breath and hopped the extra foot up, successfully grabbing the gutter. She slid sideways around the round face of the building until she found a downspout, which she shimmied down hand-over-hand to the ground floor. Before moving on, she marked carefully where her entrance was by finding several tall buildings to orient herself by.

Then she ran. Alene was a good runner. Her slippers had suede soles that allowed a quiet run with good traction. She typically was able to wear them for a week at a time before needing to break out a new pair, so she bought them as stock for a fictitious business, a hundred at a time.

She made good time as she backtracked towards the complex that held the places she'd visited earlier in the evening. A quick look when the Ivon's Tower showed - no lights on in the upper floors; he wasn't likely there. She sprinted on through a neighborhood their company had skirted, thinking it would be a good shortcut.

It was Alene's first trip through the Dives, not a place a respectable young woman would want to be seen out alone after dark. But Alene had no intention of being seen by anyone, respectable or not. Here where the rooflines were less steep, she tried elevating her position. The problem up here became the relatively poor repair that these buildings were in, and she dropped a tile more than once.

When vaulting the space between two buildings, she caught a glimpse of three men menacing a fourth. She paused, then headed back quietly to observe. The biggest man shoved the victim into a pile of garbage in the alley, and demanded "the stuff". One of the other men turned to act as a lookout, while the third drew a slim dagger.

The tile Alene grabbed slipped out easily. It weighed a couple of pounds, and she aimed for the one with the knife. He was just starting to speak when his head dropped to the ground before the rest of him crumpled. The big man looked down at his friend, concerned, realizing the issue too late to dodge Alene's next missile.

The lookout turned back to see the victim standing over his unconscious friends, and he ran for it. When the victim looked up, he saw no one. Nor would he, as Alene was already two buildings over. She skillfully ran and leapt from one rooftop to the next, unnoticed until she ran into another person moving along the rooftops unseen.

He stepped out from behind a chimney, pulling a sooty rope out of the top. She barreled into him at a full run, bouncing off and catching herself on the mortared bricks. The cat burglar fell onto his butt, sliding down the blue tiles, grabbing for any handhold. The ropes zipped back into the chimney, a loud crash heard several floors below as his loot bag burst at the hearth.

The burglar flipped over the edge with a broken section of corroded guttering and hung for dear life several floors up. Lamps were lit in a dozen windows, as people rose to address the ruckus. Once again, Alene was already several rooftops away. She orienteered her way to the Library, plotting her return route as she went.

It took a few moments to determine where to gain access to the roof, but she found a stucco building built against the stone wall of the Library that allowed her a path. Once up, she found decades worth of ignored care. In a few places, the moon glinted off of glass, exposed under lichen. She took a moment to scrape a portion of one pane of glass clean enough to observe.

The scene wasn't much different from this vantage, except that no one was looking in her direction. She poked around several panes with different vantage points, with one realization – Johan was not there. She crept on, along the edges of the building, crossing the top of the sidewall around the courtyard to the greenhouse.

This glass had been maintained better, almost like there was a dedicated caretaker. She took a much faster route here, along a stone catwalk with glass panels on either side. While the plants were beautiful, there was only one person in there this late, and it was not Johan. Alene moved on to the Palace of Lights.

Here the courtyard was darkened, as the city neared its sleepiest state. No performers, no stagehands, no actors – just the little old man with a broom. She ran and climbed and jumped her way back to the apartments, where she found a furious Beatrice waiting when she swung in from the gutter.

Her guards had scattered, searching the city for their charge. Johan was searching the city, too. Alene was tired now, adding to her frustration and disappointment. She changed and cleaned up, and fell asleep, exhausted.

Chapter 48

Bring the Heat

The dwarves of the Argentine, Aureate, and Smaragdine Holts entered the Palace of Lights early. They found the seats that were assigned to them with the help of a young man in white with a blue apron. The dwarves at first teased each other about the overstuffed cushions on their chairs, but settled on using them to ensure they could see in the midst of the crowd. They took in the details of the sets that surrounded them, discussing how this or that worked.

"Remember those columns we passed in the entryway?" said Angus, who had joined the other dwarves after their tour. "I think they are hollow."

"They didn't look like the best stone," agreed Drailin. "But why would they be hollow?"

"We are here early enough to see for certain," answered Angus, pointing at the upper, open area of the courtyard. "In a little while, the night sky will disguise those wires we see. The actors, or some of them, appear to fly above our heads. They are counterweighted by weights that run up and down in those columns, tuned to each actor's weight and what they are doing."

"Interesting. There must be miles of this wire. Where do they get it?" asked Thannon.

"That's a great question. I have no idea. But we can ask Johan when he's around."

A server walked up and greeted them.

"Welcome to the Palace of Lights, my good dwarves. I wonder what I can get for you this early evening?" There was only a little emphasis on the word "early", not quite enough for true rudeness. But the message came across clearly.

"Sausages and seed cakes, perhaps?" The voice was clear and melodious, and belonged to Johan, with a hand on Artemus' and Floin's shoulders.

"We don't have those things in the kitchen, sire," said the server, "but we could acquire them for you."

"Nonsense," offered Johan, "what do you have ready now, that wouldn't put you in a bad spot?"

"We do have extra N'gri, sire."

"N'gri it is. Extra sauce, if you please!"

As the server nearly ran to the kitchen, the older dwarves chuckled.

"That young man knows his place, doesn't he?" laughed Drailin.

"I'd say he does," agreed Artemus, "and extra sauce? You are too kind, Johan!" The King winked at the Ivon, who inclined his head in deference.

"The entertainment will be a while yet, so this seemed a likely diversion." He looked at the next table. "Alene did not join you, then?"

"I understand she was out late last night, Johan." Angus narrowed his eyes. "I would have expected you had something to do with that."

"Not this time. Our ships passed in the night, and we never saw one another. Please send her my sincere greetings. Oh, here come your appetizers. I have to finish with the preparations. Enjoy!"

The Ivon Nova jogged away, disappearing into the maze of sets and lights that described this unique place.

Minutes later the server returned with two armloads of plates, each with several multi-colored and layered cylinders of mostly rice with vegetables and fish inside. Two lines of dots ran side by side on each square plate. After one of each was placed with utmost care in front of the dwarves, the server offered two slender sticks to each as utensils.

Artemus took one like a quill and supported the other in the crook of his thumb, pinched a section of the N'gri, dipped it in two of the gradated sauce dots, and poised it whole into his mouth with confidence. Drailin did the same, with a surprising flourish of the sticks.

Angus looked very closely at how Artemus had lined up his sticks, and made a passable imitation. With just a little sauce, he was able to maneuver one of the large bites into his mouth as well. The taste was better than he remembered, a fine mix of crunch and softness and flavor that melted in his mouth. He smiled as he chewed.

Thannon struggled with his sticks, giving up after a failed attempt and grabbing the runaway N'gri with his fingers and drenching it in sauce. Floin skipped the sticks altogether and the two popped sauce-laden bites into their mouths. Angus tried to say something through his full mouth, but Artemus kicked him under the table with a significant look.

Both of the finger-feeders looked at each other with wide, teary eyes; inhaling through suddenly drippy sinuses. The older dwarves laughed for a long time about that.

"Sorry, da, I tried to warn you." Angus' face showed that he really was sorry.

"I'm not!" Artemus laughed. "Do you know how rarely we get to see dwarves learn this lesson? This is the most fun I've had in weeks!"

Chapter 49

Our Names in Lights

The Palace of Lights filled up with guests that filtered in one group after another. Each group was led to an assigned table with little pomp and less chaos. Every step of this evening had been rehearsed to perfection, starting with mundane activities like these. The wait staff knew where people were assigned, what they were likely to order, personal preferences, and even challenges.

By an hour after sundown, the dining floor and surrounding plazas were as full as the night had grown dark. The Palace was lit brilliantly from inside, of course. Several courses of traditional Ivonian food were served and enjoyed, with several courses of drinks to go with it.

Ynghild personally sat Alene and her party, not far from the dwarves, and disappeared into the crowd. Alene wore a stoic scowl, obviously still upset but not being loud about it. The dwarves waved at her when they caught her attention, eliciting a momentary smile and return gesture.

The cacophony of a thousand conversations hushed as the lights all dimmed at once, the most visible thing an unblocked view of the night sky. Soft, ethereal music emanated from tubes hidden around the courtyard, piping sound played by an orchestra in another room entirely. The lightplay was a clean experience for the listener, and Johan liked it that way.

Clever valves on the tubes opened and closed, granting the ethereal music a swirling quality that led the viewer's attention in one direction, then another. Four bright lanterns produced beams of light that swirled with the music, fully drawing the crowd's attention. After a minute, the light beams focused on a balcony, rising slowly to reveal Johan, the Ivon Nova.

"Thank you for coming, one and all. As many of you are aware, I am Johan C'Antrell, the Ivon Nova. The Nova portion of my title is now somewhat worn, indicating 'new', but it still applies. And that transition is the center of why we are here tonight - to honor and recognize the people who made it all happen.

"But first I want to remind us all of why we made this change. The Ivon Prior ruled over several decades of relative prosperity and peace. Complaints were few, until the last few years. He raised taxes. He insisted on more and more people and products from the surrounding areas. He conspired with Jean DePet to annex Veynsport, creating East Ivonsport.

"At sea, he caused competing ships to be interdicted and slaves taken, with the remaining crew burned to the waterline along with their ships. Inland, he sent an armed force to the farming community of Pentref, where he caused the whole town to be murdered and their bodies desecrated to act as an example. Patrick, would you and your company stand, to be recognized as the people who took revenge on the murderers of Pentref? Well done Patrick and company." Johan paused for applause.

"The Ivon Prior made a deal with a powerful orc to cause trouble along the borders. For the first time in decades, orcs caused problems for us south of the mountains and east of the river. And as I will explain later, that powerful orc would come back to hurt us in a big way.

"And then, he started losing. He lost the battle to keep East Ivonsport, where humans, orcs, and dwarves took part. Hundreds of Ivonian citizens. Hundreds of Veynsian citizens. Much of the town of East Ivonsport. Dwarves, and even goblins, lost their lives. And that says nothing of the orcs who were compelled to attack.

"If you were there at the battle of East Ivonsport, please stand so we can recognize you." Patrick again stood with several men. Thannon, Angus, and Alene, with several of her guards. And a dozen individuals sprinkled throughout the crowd. Applause once again filled the space.

"I nearly lost my life in that battle, as did a good friend, Angus. Wave for the crowd, Angus. This dwarf helped me enter the fray against unwinnable odds, and we carried the night, but it took a great healer, Indaria, to save us. Unfortunately, it appears Indaria is not here with us this evening. But Angus, you would agree, we owe our lives to her. To Indaria! And to Angus' vorpal axe!

"That night both East Ivonsport and the vestiges of Veynsport died. Out of the ashes rose Canolbwynt Masnach and Cam Makinesi, twin cities that usher in a new era of productive society. The leaders of those settlements are here with us tonight, right over there…"

Johan went on to enumerate a dozen actions and events that led up to the point of the recent battles at the city of Ivonal itself. He recognized people from each, and made sure to thank others for their parts much more than glorify his own. He paused and let the crowd go silent before diving in.

"And now for the most difficult part. Several months ago, all of this came to a head, like a lurking volcano. That pent-up energy blew right here in our own beloved city. The Lightplay you are about to see encompasses several days that proved to be pivotal and costly for our city and nation, and even the lands surrounding.

"But I think that, like a tree that grows stronger after a heavy pruning, we will all be the better for it. Now for the heroes of this play, a quick acknowledgement: King Thannon, of the Smaragdine Holt, who led the contingent of dwarves that pulled Angus from the belly of the beast. Queen Alene of the Veyns, who prevented a large naval battle with a critical action in the harbor. Patrick Smith, leader of Gymdeithas Fasnach, who stood at the battle of the North Green. My Second, Ynghild, who stood with me in the tower at the fateful moment, and Angus Dragonbane, who saved us all from the ravages of the dragon queen Uvrede the Deposed with an impossible attack."

The standing ovation lasted several minutes, stopped by Johan asking for calm.

"It is time now, to see the Lightplay honoring these people and their deeds, and the whole city that had their different parts. Please enjoy with me, "Potentia per Sanguinem!"

Chapter 50

Potentia per Sanguinem

The Palace of Lights went dark. This was not the kind of dark where you notice the footlights and the stray candle in the corner. Rather, a pure blackness that left only the stars above, and even those appeared black while eyes adjusted. Before those stars were even fully visible again, a rustling sound like a bedsheet being shaken flat onto a bed surrounded the courtyard.

As that noise and a little breeze subsided, a picture of the darkened harbor showed on one corner of the building, while a flying model of the Veynsian Royal Yacht arrived. An athletic Angel, dressed as Alene, walked in midair, as if she was heading from the ship down the docks towards the city, presenting herself to the night guard. Other suspended actors ferried barrels in, setting them in a ponderous stack behind her.

"Alene" was arrested, bound, and carried into the city while the Yacht sailed away, leaving the barrels. Then orange, red, and yellow streamers exploded from the barrels like a firework, flapping like fire to indicate the burning of much of the harbor. The scene faded out.

The Ivon's Tower, looming far above on the southern wall - a pantomime version of the Ivon Prior screamed in grief and horror, shaking his fists at the harbor. The spotlight faded and shrank, swept down the tower and across a prop wall eastward, drawing the eye.

The eastern wall lit up with an ethereal line drawing that resolved into a scene of the Greenway, all yellow fields and people harvesting. That scene faded away as a new light illuminated the northern panel.

This scene depicted a harvest festival at the Greenway, replete with happy faces, marriage proposals, dances and fireworks. The music from the unseen orchestra depicted the same, while the

Narrator, played by Johan, told the story of the great harvest, leading to the untimely deaths of Willm and Zane.

The next scene showed the people of the nascent group Gymdeithas Fasnach gathering an army and training. They were shown marching to the North Green and setting their lines. The scene then changed again, always transferring in an order from left to right, bringing the crowd into the barracks, where the meaning of the green sashes was discussed.

This process repeated, bringing the focus to the coastal countryside to the east of the city, which expanded the vignette to find the road circling around three edges of the building. From the dark western wall came a shrieking whistle, and a flying land train that continued the whistle all the way around the space, disappearing again into the dark.

On the wall opposite where the train disappeared, a scene of the late King Bedwyn, loading the great steam-powered bolt launcher on the back of the now-static train. The Eastgate was projected opposite, and Johan narrated Bedwyn's original intentions to bring down the gates (or the wall) with the barbed and chained bolt.

The scene changed to show the Northgate on one wall, and the North Green opposite. The lights came up, revealing hundreds of people dressed as militia on the Green side, and a similar amount on the gate side, lined up to fight. The Ivonians charged the militia, running between and over tables with battlecries. Half of the attackers paused in a line, still standing on tables in many cases.

As the smaller Ivonian force engaged the larger militia, the green sashes attacked the blue-clad Ivonians from behind, and in a few seconds, the green sashes joined the militia while the "bodies" of slain Ivonians were dragged out of sight. They left a red chalky substance as they were taken[14].

For the first time in memory, the fastidious wait staff were not instantly there to clean stains, right glasses, or remove the dishes and food scattered by the ruckus.

The lights faded away as the scene changed again, depicting the Eastgate and a barn, when a hundred shining dwarves charged from the steam wagon. They tromped along using a hedge as

14 A keen-eyed observer might have noted that while the fallen writhed in their death-throes, they opened these powdered chalk packets between themselves and the tables, chairs and floors. Johan spent a great deal of time on this effect, wanting to fully convey the real prices of wars on those that most often insisted upon them.

cover, trying to get to a big barn to lie in wait. Their armor shone vibrantly. The impression was of an impregnable unit with massive power.

The space above the Eastgate exploded, a real fireball rising into the night sky. The Eastgate opened, a fiery cavalry charging straight at the barn. From the dissipating fireball emerged a grand dragon rig, the largest moveable prop ever made for the lightplays. It flew over the charging cavalry and incinerated them, then turned towards the barn.

The shiny dwarves were ready to face the dragon and die in flames when the steam wagon blew its whistle. Uvrede turned and charged it, and Bedwyn loosed the bolt. The sky above Uvrede's head ignited as a dozen flamethrowers blew burning alcohol into the air, giving the illusion that the space around the wagon was engulfed in flames. When the flash subsided, both the wagon and the dragon were missing.

The shiny dwarves charged the Eastgate, meeting no resistance, and that portion faded out. Back on the floor, Gymdeithas Fasnach's army stood in a line to the north. An armored column of Ivonian heavy soldiers lined the south wall. The Ivonians charged again, and the flame effect ran from east to west above, drawing the eye upwards long enough to see that the heavies had all crouched down under ash-colored cloaks.

The Ivon's death scene played out in a balcony on the south, just at the base of the tower. "Johan" stabbed the "Ivon" in the neck, hovering face-to-face with his victim. Johan spoke the dreadful words with the same passion he had on the day.

"I take your life as payment for the evil you did. I take your life for the evil you made me and Ynghild and Brennan and so many more do. I take your life for what you made me into."

As the actor finished his death scene, Ynghild played herself and acknowledged the transfer of power in the same way.

"That's not all you take. You take his crown."

"Johan" produced an oversized version of the banner the Ivon Prior had kept, and unfurled it over the railing, reading the words out loud.

"Potentia per Sanguinem!" he shouted.

"Potentia per Sanguinem!" echoed the cast, every one facing the tower and kneeling.

Johan, as the Narrator, heard the saying echoed from the crowd as well, and noted some of the audience kneeling toward the faux Ivon Nova. Some of the more astute did the same towards the Director's balcony Johan had been speaking from. He glanced back at his guards and assistant directors.

"Ready for the big finish? It's not long now!"

The actors in the balcony, including the "Ivon Nova," jumped to their feet as the giant Uvrede puppet flew by at eye level. The "Ivon Nova" lamented the need for a dragonslayer, to which "Angus" broke the fourth wall and grinned at the audience, "I wonder where we could find one of those?"

"Angus" finished with an exaggerated wink, and the "Ivon Nova" tossed him a long, double ended spear, which he spun in expert ways. The spotlight that illuminated them dimmed and ran up the tower as a pinpoint, showing "Angus" magically at the top of the tower, still spinning that overlong spear.

Then the whole place shook with a roar generated by the unseen orchestra. Yellow and red lights and streamers popped twenty feet up from the floor, subsiding to reveal Uvrede's head at the base of the tower, rising as if the dragon was climbing. Several people screamed in surprise.

Their attention was drawn above to "Angus" again, who shouted, "For the Holt, and for Ivonia!" One last flourish with the spear, and "Angus" dove headfirst, spear held like a lance pointed right at the climbing dragon puppet. Uvrede the Deposed, legendary dragon of yore, was unfazed, and roared again as she opened her mouth to swallow the "dwarf" and his lance whole.

A powerful gust of wind blasted the crowd, just on the verge of knocking people over, as the whole Uvrede assembly took off and flew over the Eastgate, another rooftop fireball erupting over the place where the dragon disappeared. The crowd roared with approval, applauding Angus' sacrifice.

Chapter 51

Potentia Perpetua

The guards outside fell to a well-timed misdirection. A young girl screamed in the hallway just out of sight, right at the moment that Vincent Lamoureux de Canape's fastest men were walking by. The guards turned to face the sound, as a decent person does, exposing their backs for split-second backstabs from practiced killers. They fell with little noise, and the scream was covered by the sound of the Dragon's roar outside.

Four men slipped into the chamber behind the director's balcony, two for each of Johan's remaining guards. Vincent stepped into the dark chamber, long, slim sword drawn. The Dragon flew away, and the spotlights converged on the director's balcony. Johan responded to a slight prick from Vincent's sword at his back as Vincent spoke into the amplification tube.

"Bravo, Johan! Another fine performance in a long string of fine performances! You, sir, are a consummate bard, a peerless actor, and flamboyant storyteller. Am I wrong?"

Vincent jabbed the sword tip in slightly when Johan went to reply, instead continuing his tirade.

"So much of what you have told us already is no more than stories. You've masked the systematic dismantling of the Angels intelligence network as a prelude to this immense show, glorifying you and your friends as heroes. But we know what actually went on.

"You waited until the Ivon Prior was distracted by the dragon and snuck in, murdering his guards and him. Is that not true?" He jostled the sharp point with that last phrase, causing a trickle of blood to run down Johan's back.

"I can see how you see it that way, Vincent. We did ascend the tower in stealth. And the Ivon was concerned about a battle and a dragon happening at the same time. But he was killed in combat, not murdered."

Johan stole a glance behind him, the room had been cleared except for him, Vincent, and two armed guards. He, of course, was armed with a conducting baton only, probably not enough.

"I respect what you are trying to do here, however." Johan projected his voice into the amplifier and beyond. "You've waited until I was distracted, murdered my guards and attacked me from behind. Bravo yourself!"

"Let's talk about what you've done, Johan, since becoming the Ivon Nova. You've given our stores and our coin to people who decided to secede. You've destroyed the largest intelligence operation in the history of the Cyfandir. You've wasted our money on this gross extravagance. And for what? All to be the best storyteller in history?

"What a tremendous waste. You, sir, are a fraud and an abuser. I should set the dogs to work on you. But at least I can set this right. I alone know how this city, this nation, indeed the whole Cyfandir should be run. And what better time than right after you have shown the world what these words mean?" He laughed a wicked laugh.

"Potentia - Potential or Advancement. Per - by or through. Sanguinem - Blood, in a very direct way. Advancement through Blood."

While Vincent was reaching his own climax, several of the flying angels had started to swing by, getting closer looks. Johan noticed, and knew his chances were low. As Vincent pulled his sword back to make a deadly thrust, Johan jumped off the balcony, intercepting a passing acrobatic Angel in a midair tackle.

As the two overbalanced the weights on the other side of the building, they fell to the floor at a controlled speed. Johan was back on his feet in a second, locating which of the audience were likely to support him, and those that might act against him. His eyes lit on the dwarves, every one of which was running towards him, flattening anyone who got in their way.

Vincent was yelling.

"Potentia Per Sanguinem! His blood is on my blade! Stop him and bring him to me!"

The crowd erupted into one big brawl, with many people looking to capitalize on the opportunity to pick sides and others looking simply to stay out of the way. The dwarves, numbering about twenty all told, wrapped around Johan, Artemus, Drailin, and Thannon.

"All right, Lad, which way do you want to go?" Artemus took command, standing on a table to get his bearings.

"That way – the Gardens. We can regroup there." Johan checked the wound in his side. Painful, but not much more than skin deep. "Vincent has more in him than I gave him credit for!"

The group started to move as one, literal centuries of training in close combat more than a match for the crowd. There was fighting, but the Kings kept insisting they not kill unless absolutely necessary.

They pushed through the crowd with great success until Angus ran his shoulder into the butt of a very large man. He stopped pushing against the unpushable bulk and looked up as the man turned. A friendly face appeared and made a welcome smile.

"Angus!" Patrick smiled and offered a hand to shake. "What the hell is happening?"

"We're going that way, and you've managed to stop me – us – from getting there. Would you help us clear a path?"

"Oh, of course! EVERYBODY MOOOOOVE!" shouted Patrick, straight in the direction Angus had indicated. It wasn't a perfect solution, but that area became less populated very quickly. They moved along.

The first true combat happened a dozen steps later, when ten armed men presented themselves against twenty unarmed dwarves. They flashed Vincent's colors, wore chainmaille and bore spears. It should have been an easy win for the men with weapons. Patrick was shoved by the dwarves to end up safely in the center of the formation. The circle became a triangle, with eight unarmed dwarves facing ten men, the dwarves still advancing at a slow walk.

When one of the men got over his shock of seeing short people walking at him with amused smiles on their faces, he took a spear-poke at Drailin, the oldest and smallest of them. This seemed to amuse the other dwarves even more, and they started laughing.

The spear tip was well-aimed, and tried to occupy the same space his face had been. Had been, because Drailin dodged to the side at the last second. He slid the back of one hand along the still-stabbing spear-shaft, grabbing with the other. A deft movement and slight pull later, and the spear was in Drailin's hands. Without hesitating, Drailin slapped the haft of the spear once on each bridge of the man's feet, breaking bones in painful ways.

Another deft move saw that same haft flex side to side, smacking the ears of the two men next to Drailin's first victim. Each involuntarily dropped their grip with one hand to cup a painful ear, and then Angus and another dwarf had spears, too. Now eight faced seven; the dwarves walked on.

A soldier tried a thrust against Angus, who used his spear, his preferred weapon until this year, to intercept and redirect the blow up and behind, where it would be above the other dwarves' heads.

Patrick yelled "Watch it!" as he grabbed the haft just behind the tip and held it a second, before jabbing it back into his attacker's face, causing a fourth man to crumple to the ground and out of the fight.

The remaining six seemed able to do basic math and retreated at the same pace as the dwarven triangle constantly advanced towards the tall wooden doors that led to the large, stone vestibule behind. Backed against the doors, the men again stood and readied to fight. One of Vincent's men rapped his spear butt against the left door in a rhythmic pattern and looked over at his remaining friends.

The other smiled, and as the door opened, they split into two groups of three and spanned either side of the ten-foot-wide doors that opened to expose a line of men in heavy armor marching up the stairs towards them. Now the spearmen acted as flankers and harassed the dwarves at the corners of their triangular formation.

On the left, three spears came at once for Siggurd, who rolled and dropped under them into a forward somersault, rising with his arms wide. He trapped all three spears together, clapped his hands above his head, then turned and trapped all three under one arm. Once their spears were useless, the dwarves from either side of Siggurd ran up and started pummeling the three, starting with low blows and leg sweeps. Siggurd redistributed the spears to the dwarves on the front line.

On the right, Denmar took a different tack; three spears came, but spaced a half second apart. He stepped back, barely out of reach, while the dwarves on either side of him grabbed the spears closest and wrestled for control. Denmar kicked the third spear from underneath, and the soldier holding it felt the full shock of the reverberation through the shaft.

With a line of spears, the task became more do-able, and the dwarves advanced to the top of the stairway as the heavily armored men reached the first step. Dwarves who had spent no more than a year or two mastering the spear ably found chinks in the armor and drove their points home. Cheaply-made spearpoints broke on cheaply-made armor, but blunt sticks worked well for pushing tall men in armor over – and down stairs.

Moments later, Patrick bludgeoned the last of these into unconsciousness. Dwarves and men picked through weapons and armed themselves just as another large wave of attackers appeared at the giant doorway they had just come through. Close to a hundred men and women in various states of armor and armament lined up and charged down the stairs.

"They are here for me, not you," Johan said to the dwarves. "I'm leaving through there. Slow them down, but don't die over this. I'm fine. Stick around, I'll see you soon!"

He ran up the next set of stairs to the wooden door. He reached for the handle as a crossbow bolt stuck just above it, pulling his hand back for a second before rushing into the Royal Gardens. He closed the door and ran inside. Artemus, Drailin, and Angus ran with him.

"Thannon will hold that line," shouted Artemus to Johan. "He's got a knack for it like his father."

They ran through the zig-zagged walkways to reach the other end before hearing men enter the gardens behind them, shouting battlecries. Thannon's stand hadn't lasted as long as they'd hoped. Johan led the dwarves over a little bridge to the large doors on the other side of the arboretum and opened one.

"All right, you youngsters can go on. Artie and I will hold this door," instructed Drailin without asking. "But make haste, we've got our limits, too."

"Thank you, gents. Like I said, stick around. I'll be back shortly." Johan jibed. He sounded more optimistic this time, like he knew he was going to make it.

"Drailin," said Angus, "Artie. It has been an honor."

"Don't push your luck, Hero." Artemus said with a wink as Angus turned away smiling.

Chapter 52

What Good is an Elf?

The door closed behind Angus and Johan, leaving Drailin and Artemus to hold a small bridge over the water that crossed the building here.

"Ah, I see it from here!" Drailin shouted. "I knew it had to be, but it took standing right here to see it!"

"What do you see, Drailin?"

"This is an artesian well, not a stream. Comes up right there. It must be how they keep so many plants and trees growing here. This kind of garden usually takes an elf!"

The dwarves heard a feminine voice laughing in the wind. They looked around for the source, and found Dar, dressed all in black, sitting in the crook of the ancient oak tree in front of them. She fit in perfectly with the tree and the rest of her surroundings.

"Dar?" asked Artemus. "There is a fight coming. You shouldn't be in here!"

"Clear out, child!" Drailin called. "Take the door behind us! It isn't safe here!"

"My dear dwarves," giggled the young woman in front of them, "there isn't a safer place for me in Ivonal!"

Another soldier, this one again wearing Vincent's colors, ran around the corner towards the dwarves, charging with a large mace held over his head. He started a battle shout, made a scary face, and… tripped on an unseen tree root that popped through the paving stones. He went from full run to unconscious, his face taking a lot of the impact.

The next tried to shortcut the back-and-forth nature of the path, jumping through a bush with brilliant flowers. As he emerged through the creeping tendrils, his momentum shifted. His feet came off the ground as he was pulled back into the bush by his neck, only his kicking feet visible with no sound for a few seconds until they went limp. The still body was gently lowered to the ground.

This process was repeated for several minutes, until a breathless Thannon and company came forward to meet the elder dwarves. They were unmolested by the Garden, and Dar never changed her smile.

"Near a hundred got by us!" Thannon was gobsmacked. "It looks like you took them all out, but you appear unharmed."

"It wasn't us," replied Artemus. "I think it was her!"

"Dar?" Asked Floin. "She's just a girl!"

"Tell him, Dar," Drailin insisted. "You aren't just a girl, are you?"

"In some very important ways, I am just a girl. But you mentioned that a place like this needs an elf. It has been a long time since one of us was here. And, like most mortals, you've exaggerated, Thannon. Your father wouldn't have. There were sixty-two that came into the garden here. Not a hundred.

"Sixty was a very important number for me. I have paid my debt to Angus and Johan with that number, as they recently slew sixty men to save mine, and Alene's."

"You paid that debt by saving them with the Dreamvine, milady," Floin stated. "You needn't have bloodied your hands this way."

"If only that were true, friend Floin. The Dreamvine always has a price. It left a mark on your son and Johan as much as it has me." She twirled a lock of green hair from under her black wig. "For all of us, the color change is the smallest bit."

"We're grateful," Artemus responded. "And we'll talk more later about it. But for now, let's see if they escaped or if they still need help!"

Chapter 53

Here Comes the Cavalry!

Johan and Angus ran out the door and down the steps to the next vestibule, the one that separated the Gardens from the Library. Johan grabbed Angus and showed him a side door, which they opened. They hurried through the dim hall a hundred feet, and they popped out into an alleyway. The street was illuminated by the Palace of Lights to one side, and the Dives were visible in the other direction.

Johan took them toward the Dives. *What a fun twist of fate*, the thought, *to be here again, evading pursuit. Maybe my life isn't totally boring after all!* They ran along the main road, away from the milling, chaotic crowds and towards the dingy debauchery of Johan's old haunts.

"I think we made it, Angus!"

"Have we though?"

Three large horses with the Dark Patrol, two blocks down, pursued them.

"What about them?" Angus asked, pointing.

"Run!" Johan replied, already a dozen strides ahead.

Angus ran, but within a block, the horsemen passed them and turned around in front of a building with multi-tiered blue awnings.

"Halt! You are under arrest!"

"I am not!" yelled the Ivon Nova. "You can see who I am!"

"I know who you were. But Vincent and I go way back. I was hoping we'd get a crack at you! I'll get a command for bringing you in!"

"You haven't brought us in yet." Johan flourished the short sword he'd lifted from one of Vincent's fallen men. "And I don't think you will."

Angus flourished his scavenged spear as well. The two adjacent Patrolmen revealed the crossbows resting on their pommels, loaded and cocked.

"Lay down your arms or I can drag your corpses to the Palace of Lights."

"I don't want to." Johan affected a pouty, sulk, something like Vincent would have done.

"Suit yourself. Shoot them in the heart. Royals, every one, absolutely useless when it comes down to it!"

The two men lifted the crossbows to make their shots when the first bent his neck at an odd angle, bolt bouncing off the cobblestones between Johan and Angus. That soldier was still falling to the ground when the second flew off his horse sideways, his bolt launching into the darkness high above.

Angus took advantage of the surprised leader and ran his spear into the lead man's face, the only part unarmored. An effective move, but unpleasant. Angus didn't retrieve the spear, rather let it fall to the ground with the corpse.

"Royalty is useless, huh?" laughed a lithe figure now astride the second rider's horse. "That's not a very nice thing to say."

"He won't say it again," Angus offered. I was hoping that was you."

"Who else would it be?" asked Johan. "Dark clothes, jumping from roof to roof. Saving heroes from thugs. Sounds like a queen to me."

"Very funny." Alene laughed, letting a street lantern illuminate her face. "Now mount up so we can get out of here!"

"No, thank you. I don't do horses." Angus waved his hands declining. "However, I can offer a little misdirection. You two go on, I'll give you a bit of cover then go in to check on my Da."

Johan picked a horse and mounted it, and the two rode off into the night. Angus held on to the third, apologizing to it. He strung together the spurs and belt items from the dead riders, and hung them from straps behind the saddle so they dangled down behind it. With a slap and a yell, the horse was running in the opposite direction, screaming and whinnying as it ran, attacked by unseen enemies behind.

Angus watched the horse clatter down the cobbles, sparks flying from steel shoes, until it left around a corner, then walked back up the stairs to the Gardens. There he listened at the grand doors for signs of life. To his relief, Floin was laughing along with the rest of the dwarves he'd left behind, chatting with the young human they'd brought along.

"We were just coming to check on you, boy!" Floin was ecstatic. "Did Johan get to safety?"

"I think so. We ran into help outside, and just in time. For a moment, it looked like we were caught."

"Should we be out there helping?" Artemus asked.

"They are away. I'd like to see what chaos is happening back in the Palace. How is everyone so relatively unbroken? I don't see much more than I'd expect in a dustup at a tavern."

"Some who attacked us weren't as lucky." offered Drailin. "And what is this about sixty men?"

"That's an odd number to come up with, Drailin," Angus inquired.

"T'weren't me, lad. The lass mentioned it. Said she were payin' you back."

Angus looked at the young human in the tree. The one removing a dark wig and showing her entirely green hair to go with her vivid green eyes.

"Have we met?" he asked, visibly wrestling to put the parts together.

"No," she answered, "and yes. When we last met, we were less complete versions of ourselves, but now we are both… more." Dar slipped gracefully out of the tree, walking smoothly across the underbrush to meet him face to face. She touched the green lock in his beard. "In a way, we are the same now, though neither of us will ever be the same."

"Dar. In-dar-ia." Angus was ashamed to have missed the connection and overjoyed to find her alive. "How did you escape–"

She put a finger across his lips.

"Later. We still have work to do. Let's go see what is happening back at the Palace of Lights. We should keep Vincent talking and give Johan time to plot his return."

"Amazing." Artemus stammered. "I never suspected. I'll never tell an elven joke again."

"My father was very impressed with you," said Thannon. "He counted you as a valuable ally. I hope to do the same in his stead."

Indaria inclined her head slightly, and walked along the path back to the vestibule that separated the Garden from the Palace. It meandered a half mile, littered with corpses of Vincent's allies, all in odd positions where they had encountered green death.

A forearm hovered above a lumpy lawn, its hand contorted. A leg hung from a fold in an oak's bark, foot and all. Several root balls held suspicious bulges that had not been there before. Bushes were thickened with dark, unmoving shapes. The sixty-two were a part of the Royal Gardens, permanently.

The dwarves, now aware of what had happened, vacillated between respect for the power the elf wielded and terror of the same. Angus made the same note Artemus had, to never tell those jokes, and do everything he could to shield Indaria from similar attempts at humor.

They found Patrick, standing alone at the top of the stairs, a smith's hammer in hand. Half a dozen foes lay at his feet. His visage was grim; no other men tried to get by him.

"I failed you all. So many slipped past." He seemed to take it personally.

"Lad, you did great," Drailin offered. "Just take a peek at what those that got by you had to deal with."

Patrick did, while the dwarves picked their way down into the vestibule. He came back quickly.

"How did that happen? Why take the time to wrap them up in plants like that?"

The dwarves laughed. Angus pointed at Indaria.

"Remember "Dar"? Remember Indaria, the elven singer I brought through the Sliver a few months ago? One and the same. She's largely responsible for those messes in there."

"Ah." Patrick visibly processed the obvious magic that had not entered his life before this point. "Thank you, I think? Or maybe, please don't kill us all?"

"I'll think about it." Dar laughed.

Chapter 54

Proper Preparation Prevents…

Johan tossed the reins to a groom in the stables, and Alene did the same.

"Where are the men I checked these horses out for?" the groom asked.

"They won't be coming back." The Ivon Nova replied. "They were up to no good and ran afoul of someone they underestimated."

"She underestimated herself," Alene added. "That won't happen again."

They ran into the tack room and down to the tunnels used by the Angels. Alene continued past where Johan stopped.

"You'll like this, it is new." He pressed a brick into the wall as if it were not mortared in place, stopping halfway. A crevice was revealed, and with a deft finger motion, a section of the wall leaned away into the space.

"You've hidden the entrance to your "elevator"! I love the spycraft!"

"I thought you'd like that. Let's go. Grab the far harnesses, the ones that look dusty. The clean ones are boobytrapped."

A few moments later, they sailed upwards, ascending the several hundred feet of the tower without a heavy breath. At the top they dropped into the Ivon's quarters, where Johan dressed for battle, a thick gambeson with chainmaille over. Alene looked over the items in his armory, lamenting the fact that his armor choices would not fit.

They both strapped on swords and daggers, and Johan added a cape in his colors. Alene laughed.

"I thought you were against capes!"

"I am – most of the time. This is one of those rare moments that will be better with a cape. Do you trust me?"

"About the cape? No."

He walked to the edge of the balcony and looked over, the Palace of Lights clearly bright several hundred yards away and a hundred or more feet down. He made something that looked like a magician's hand gestures in the dark.

"I mean do you really trust me?"

"More than ever."

"Then come here and kiss me. For luck."

The Queen complied, wrapping her arms around his neck. He wrapped an arm around her, kissed her, and jumped.

They fell for a second, catching ten feet down and sliding away from the tower, Alene wrapped around Johan, arms and legs squeezing him tight. His cape rippled dramatically behind them. They whizzed down the dwarven-made cable straight toward the Palace of Lights.

Johan was ready to take his throne back from the momentary usurper Vincent, and show him the meaning of Potentia Per Sanguinem.

Chapter 55

Entirely Sanguine

The dwarves came back in to find a slimmer crowd, some non-political folks having left the building when the fighting started, and over a hundred dead and more than that wounded. Those that supported Vincent were gathered under the Director's Balcony where Vincent Lamoureux de Canapes stood pontificating about his victory.

Others, the dwarves included, formed a group on the far side, looking and listening with grim faces.

"Not long from now, we will have the body of the coward Johan, pretender to the Ivon's throne. Here you see his blood on my sword," Vincent held the sword aloft as proof. "If he returns alive, I still advance through blood, as he fled combat!"

"Di ye thin hill dae tha, yoong feller?" Drailin turned on his best Duibni impression.

"What?"

"Di ye thin hill retorn alie?"

Vincent looked puzzled, and annoyed. Artemus stepped in.

"Artemus here. King Artemus, if that helps. Drailin wants to know if you think that the Ivon Nova will return alive?"

"Ah. No. I've seen to it."

"'Ave ye? Ow? Ye bin ere!" Drailin stifled a chuckle.

"You are unintelligible. What is he saying?"

"Oh," Artemus helped, "he wants to ask how you've seen to it he won't come back alive. Seeing how you've been here and all."

"My men are set all around the building and will interdict him."

"Wot," interjected Drailin, "so's ye can 'ave inothah go?"

Vincent looked expectantly again to Artemus, who stood in a group with ten other dwarves.

"My good friend here suggests that you might intend to bring the Ivon Nova back here, alive, to finish your duel. Is he correct?"

"No, he is not."

"Is he on the right track?"

"So you don't want him to return?"

"No. Now if you are quite finished," Vincent replied, "I would like to move on."

"Yes sir. That sounds good," replied Artemus.

"Is it," asked Angus, "that you are afraid of him? Do you think he'd win?"

"No." replied Vincent.

"No, you aren't afraid of him? Or, no, you don't think he'll win?"

"Now, look. I've had just about enough out of you dwarves…"

"Well," shouted Floin, "we'll keep going until you've had quite enough of us."

A palpable vibration was felt overhead, building into an audible one. A low humming from one of the wires above, building higher and higher in pitch and volume. Vincent strained to locate the source, as did most of the remaining attendees.

"Is that," shouted Drailin, "a bordt? I cannae see it plain!"

"He's back," laughed Angus. "And just in time. I think Vincent was losing his patience…"

Johan and Alene flew in like the Angels on one static line, descending into the atrium and back up to slow them and allow a rooftop landing. The crowd ooh-ed and aah-ed. Alene alighted first, followed by Johan. She immediately started to shimmy down, vaulting from balcony to balcony to get to Vincent. Johan fiddled with his rigging and then ran straight out again, jumping out into the center of the atrium.

Twenty feet across, his outward progress halted as he hit the end of his tether, then he arced straight back down towards Vincent. Johan leaned back like a swing and planted both feet in Vincent's chest, driving him into the room beyond, where a guard caught the would-be usurper. They both fell to the ground.

Vincent rose, looking around at his guards, then at Johan.

"You can't hope to win, Johan. I have the advantage in numbers."

"That is how it appears. But you can't just have these guys kill me, that wouldn't allow for Potentia per Sanguinem succession."

Someone knocked at the door. One of Vincent's guards put his hand on the knob as the door exploded inward, propelled by Thannon and Denmar's boots in a coordinated stomp. The guard was carried several feet back, landing in a heap under the ruined door.

Thannon, Denmar, and four more dwarves streamed in and engaged Vincent's guards. Johan laughed and shrugged with his palms wide.

"Oh, that is much better, thank you, Thannon! Now Vincent, where were we?" He drew his sword and struck a gentlemanly combat stance next to the railing, right where he could be seen by the audience.

Vincent unsheathed the saber that still showed Johan's blood on the tip and advanced to stand next to the Ivon Nova. He looked up at the young woman standing casually on the railing behind Johan.

"Who are you supposed to be?" Vincent demanded.

"Don't mind me, I'm just a person with royal blood waiting my turn. If you defeat Johan, I'll try my hand. I'm faster than him, you know."

"I was being polite," laughed Johan, "My mother always taught me 'ladies first'."

Alene blushed and looked away, laughing.

"Hush now!" Vincent was beyond frustrated. "I'll have your sword, Johan, and your crown."

Vincent issued a thrust, which Johan parried. Johan's riposte was countered similarly, and the two exchanged attacks and defenses for a full minute before a pause. At the end of the burst, both sported crimson slashes, but nothing critical. The crowd was absolutely silent.

"You've been practicing, Vincent!" Johan said in a laudatory manner.

"I have," he replied. "I know how important this is. And you are making a reasonable accounting of yourself, too."

"I thank you, sir. I'll even forgive you for being a little prick earlier this evening. But first, I'm afraid I'll have to kill you."

They quickly scanned around the room, and found that the other fights had all been resolved, each in a different manner. Two of

Vincent's men were dead, the rest unconscious or being escorted out. Their duel was the last remaining action.

Vincent launched another flurry of strikes at Johan, who retreated a step at a time under the withering attack. Vincent smiled as he pushed his opponent all the way back to the wall. His confidence restored, Vincent took the advantage to speak.

"I've got you now! You were always his pet, when it should have been me. And you say you killed him? Right. You and what army? These dwarves?"

"Angus was there. As was Alene and Ynghild. Also, four guards and two generals. It was a fair fight. Where were you that day? Leading the troops?" Johan knew that wasn't true, Vincent had no part in the military. "Or were you watching from the safety of your tower?"

Flustered, Vincent slipped on blood he hadn't noticed and turned to stagger-run back to the other end of the room to recover. Johan made a quick move, clipping the wire from his harness to the back of Vincent's belt. He hauled backwards on the line, unbalancing Vincent and pushing him toward the railing again.

Vincent dropped his sword over the edge and yelled out for mercy. Johan kicked him in the chest, watching as he fell off the railing, screaming, only to be caught by the wire. There he hung over the crowd, twenty feet up, moaning and bleeding from several places.

Alene jumped down into the balcony and grabbed Johan's hand, raising it up for the crowd like a prize fighter celebrating his victory.

"Ivonia, who is this man?"

Those who remained in the crowd and supported Johan shouted, "Ivon Nova!" This started a rhythmic chant that cascaded through the whole place, with most of Vincent's supporters joining in as well.

Johan stepped to the edge of the balcony, holding his saber high, blood still dripping down the length.

"You all saw the Lightplay that showed the story of my rise to power. It showed how allies from diverse backgrounds can work as well or better than the monocultural automatons that people like the Ivon Prior and this joker prefer.

"Tonight, you have seen the same story play out. A challenge was made. The challenger appeared to triumph, but through the efforts of people working together, we see the challenger hanging helplessly and bleeding. Vincent Lamoureux des Canapes made a challenge, and twists above you, defeated.

"I remain the Ivon Nova."

Chapter 56

Hastened Chastening

After everyone was sent home, Johan invited Alene, Angus, and Indaria to his chambers to wind down. Most of the dwarven party was back at the tavern Johan had rented for them, celebrating their victory. The remaining dignitaries bent the knee as appropriate, recognizing Johan as the rightful Ivon Nova.

But one person stood out as missing. Ynghild. She had not been seen since the middle of the Lightplay. Now that the four friends sat on the highest balcony in Ivonal, looking over the places they had seen combat that evening, it came up.

"I didn't see your girlfriend out there," said Alene in a catty way.

"She's not – what?" Johan was flustered. "Maybe ex, if you go a long way back. But we aren't… we don't…"

"She gets a lot more of your time than I do," stated Alene.

Johan got up and headed to his liquor cabinet.

"It's her job as Second. She gets a lot done for me. What can I get for you?"

"A Veynsian red of some sort," said Alene. "Surprise me."

"Why don't you pick what you think an elf would enjoy?" teased Indaria. "We'll see how close you can get."

"Anything short and stiff will work for me, Johan. Thank you." Angus was ready for a bit of calm after the evening's excitement.

There was a knock at the door, and Johan called for the knocker to enter. It was Ynghild.

"Speak of the devil," Angus quipped. "You aren't here to try to kiss me again, are you?"

"No, not yet." Ynghild blew him a kiss and laughed, and walked directly over to Johan. "Are you alright?"

"I am. But I expected to see you earlier than this."

"I tried to catch up to you since you first left the Palace, but I kept missing."

"Did you?"

"I did. I ran after you towards the garden, then through it. That was a nightmare."

"It is good I know who you are." Indaria chuckled. "But yes, she was there."

"Thank you. I took a side exit and ran to find you on the street, but found only the three Dark Guard, motionless on the cobblestones."

"Sorry about that." Alene giggled.

"I had some hand in that business…" Angus feigned offense.

"There I was, just running my mouth…" Johan laughed. "Go on, Yng. So, you saw we were mounted…"

"I did, but I was confused when the sounds ran away from the Ivon's Tower. I was sure you'd come up here to regroup and arm yourself. But I chased the sound of horses all the way to the harbor.

"Once I was certain you hadn't gone that way, I hired a harbor coach to bring me to the Tower. I could see signs you'd been here, but you'd gone already. So, I rode the coach back to the Palace, which had just cleared out. I figured you'd be back here at some point, so I returned."

"Sounds like a busy night," said Angus. "You must be tired."

"I'm fine. Glad it looks like you all are not heavily wounded. Did someone tend your wounds, Johan?"

"Quick patches, a few stitches. Nothing deep."

"What is next for Vincent?"

"I haven't decided. I left him hanging with a guard overnight. He won't die. But do I imprison him? Interrogate him to find his accomplices? Maybe I'll turn him over to you."

"Whatever you wish. I'm uncomfortable with leaving someone who tried to kill you living."

"We could hold a trial. Make a big public deal of it. Trot out those that were loyal to him and have them make choices in public."

"That sounds risky."

"Mmm." Johan nodded. "We'll pick it up in the morning. Would you make sure Indaria gets quarters fitting her station?"

"No need," replied the elf. "I'd like to stay in the Garden. It still needs attention, and it does feel the most like home for me."

"You are welcome to it," replied Johan. "I suppose I should send a crew in to clean up."

"Oh," cautioned Indaria, "I wouldn't do that. I'll encourage the plants to clean up after themselves. They are still… on edge. This might be a bad time to have someone prune a bush to retrieve a body."

"Noted."

They drank and sat for the next hour, past midnight, talking about the evening's events and what might come next. Then Johan suggested the party might be over for the evening.

"Let's adjourn and meet in the morning. Yng, would you make arrangements at Levay Hall for a brunch for these and the other dignitaries? It would be nice to have some offerings for the different palettes."

"I'd be happy to. Good evening, all." Ynghild left via the front door.

"Can I walk you to your Garden?" Angus offered an elbow to Indaria.

"I'd be delighted. You can tell me about your Dreams." She laughed as Angus stumbled at that prompt, and they filed out the door.

"I should probably go, too," said Alene. "It's late."

"We could have a high-level meeting," Johan suggested with a wide-armed sweeping gesture. "We are, after all, heads of neighboring states."

She smiled, and walked up to him, placing one hand gently on his chest.

"Take tonight to heal. Let's see how you are feeling tomorrow." She kissed him once, and turned to leave.

Johan sent two guards to bolster her four that had been just outside the door to see her home. Then he checked his wounds again and took Alene's advice. The night was dark and short, but he was alive. He was still the Ivon Nova.

Chapter 57

Making Arrangements

Ynghild walked towards Levay Hall, but stopped by the Palace of Lights on the way. She noted the four guards spread at tables around the place Vincent hung. Vincent was asleep, and snoring, but the guards were not.

Ynghild slunk quietly up the stairs and out where the Director's Balcony lay. She crept in quietly, taking a full minute to open and shut the door behind her. From behind the railing, she dipped into her sleeve and retrieved a tube, flared at both ends. Pulling on the flares, it extended to be about two feet long.

She found a tiny vial with a stopper in her cleavage, and pulled a dart from a recess in her shoe. First, she dipped the dart in the vial, then loaded the dart into the blowgun. She slowly rose over the railing just enough for a clean shot at Vincent, and waited for his body to slowly twist so his bare back faced her.

She inhaled deeply and applied a pressurized blast of air into the dart gun, the dart sticking deeply into Vincent's back. He roused slightly from sleep with a groan, then stopped snoring. The guards traded jokes about how they appreciated him being quiet for once.

"I thought he'd never shut up!"

"I was eyeballing that brick over there. I was ready to help him sleep better!"

"I think there's something wrong with him. Nobody snores that loudly!"

"I dunno. At least when he was snoring we knew he was alive. He's not moving at all now…"

Ynghild snuck back out of the Palace of Lights and continued on to Levay Hall. She woke the Chief Cook, and they went over some dishes that should be included for the next morning. Sausages and beer for dwarves, mutton for Patrick and his backwater delegates, and some garden-y, salad-y choices for the elf. Neither of them had ever fed an elf.

----- -----

Once they were on the dark street, Indaria asked Angus probing questions about his time in the Dreamvine.

"Did you dream more, or have nightmares?"

"Oh, that is a tough question. A bit of both I'd say, but with somewhat more good points than scary."

"What parts were the most concerning?"

"At the time, I'd have said watching the arrows fall out of me. But recently…"

"Recently?"

"Recently I've had some problems. Like flashbacks."

"Like after a fight flashbacks?"

"Not exactly."

"Then like what?"

"When I touch very old things, sometimes I get an echo of what they've been through."

"Can you give me an example?"

"The first time it happened, I was at some ruins with my father. A place with stone stools set in a circle around an altar. When I touched one of the stools, I experienced what another person had, long, long ago."

"I still don't understand. Were you remembering their memories?"

"I wouldn't say 'remembering,' as such. More like I was living a moment of their lives. Each time it has happened, I remembered a moment of stress, or of excitement, or… ahem… passion."

Indaria gave Angus a moment to recover. She, of course, had not experienced anything like what Angus was describing. *Maybe that is to be expected,* she thought. *He is a dwarf, after all, and I am an elf. We should have different experiences.*

"When you have these experiences," she asked, "are you in control?"

"That might make things easier. No, I am not in control during those times. Not at all. And that fact has almost gotten me killed already."

"A dream put you in danger?"

"Aye. My body acts it out, you see. Like the Dragon Uvrede. You saw the depiction of me diving down at it, being intentionally eaten, right?"

"I did. It was a dramatic depiction of bravery."

"About that. What really happened was that Johan tossed me a long spear from the Ivon Prior's collection. I caught it, and became someone else. Something else. I knew the spear, knew it was called a Sleagh Mhòr, and how to activate its magic."

"That sounds like a good thing."

"Nay, lassie. It was a horrible thing. In my mind I was a graceful, powerful, athletic she-elf. And I knew the complex dance to make the magic happen, and I performed that dance, in its entirety."

"The elven magic dances are beautiful. I wish I could have seen it."

"My body stayed the same! This chubby frame, bearing so much evidence of a hearty dwarven diet, performed that dance. I was sore for weeks!"

"I'd hardly call that nearly killing you."

"I'm not done yet! I awoke from that dream hanging from the spear over the side of the wall on the Ivon's Tower, and as soon as I was me again I couldn't hold the pose. I *fell* into that dragon's mouth."

"Holding an activated Sleagh Mhòr."

"It was terrible!"

"It was heroic."

"But it was an accident! Whoever heard of an accidental hero?"

"Anyone who believes in things that might not be possible. This is great. You get to be a Dragonbane without the cocky attitude."

They walked on in silence for a few more steps before Angus spoke again.

"I haven't thanked you for saving me. I'm different, but I'm still here. Thank you."

"Angus, you are a special dwarf. You bear the Blessing of Sara-Tholah. I'm still not sure exactly how that Blessing will apply itself in your life, but you have done well by it already. Saving you that day, and the dance you learned in your Dreaming, led to the greatest Dragon I'm aware of being stopped from burning the city to the ground. If that is all you did, your life would be worth the price."

He felt the satchel behind his beard warm, and he placed a hand over it.

"I–uh.." he started.

"I wanted you to have it."

"What is it?"

"I won't tell you. Please keep it safe. I may ask for it back, one day. For now, I think it may guide you in times of need."

"Are you sure?"

"I've never been more sure of anything."

After another brief silence, Angus spoke again.

"What was your time in the vine like? Are you different?"

She placed a hand on her belly absent-mindedly.

"I am forever changed. In different ways than you, but still changed. I am more powerful than ever, yet more limited, too. You will see, soon enough, what I mean."

"We saw your power in the Garden, didn't we?"

Indaria grinned.

"I am only limited by the plant life around me. It is a heady feeling. And yet one that tells me I should never walk where there are no plants or animals. A desert would terrify me."

"Let's not take you to a desert then."

Chapter 58

Let's Do Brunch

Ynghild welcomed everyone into the brunch, seating them at three long tables. A simple menu was circulated at each table, with white-and-blue clad serving staff taking orders and filling them nearly as fast. Every one of the out-of-town delegates from last night was here. There was only one person missing.

Johan.

He was only five minutes late, red-faced with anger. He called Ynghild aside to have a conference. He whispered closely for a moment when she jumped back in shock.

"Dead?" she yelped with clear surprise. She came back in closer to finish the conversation.

"Yes, Vincent is dead. Poisoned in the night. The guards say he was snoring one minute, sleeping soundly the next. None saw any approach."

"Without an approach, how could he be poisoned?"

Johan looked at her with a deadpan expression.

"You have the same training as I. You know fifteen ways that could happen."

"Was he fed anything earlier? A little wine on a cloth, perhaps?"

"It doesn't matter. He's gone, and with him my reason for a large trial to smoke out collaborators."

"He's gone, and you are here. Any collaborators are going to think twice before challenging you again. Shall we join your guests?"

They came back to the table. Johan stood behind his chair and took a sip of juice before addressing the group. Near Johan sat his

Second, Queen Alene, King Thannon, King Artemus, Indaria, daughter of the Elven Speaker, and Patrick Smith, the de facto leader of Gymdeithas Fasnach.

"Thank you all again for coming. I apologize for last night's trouble. Vincent Lamoureux des Canapes will not bother us again. His wounds were worse than they appeared, and he succumbed during the night."

Johan allowed a respectful moment of silence before resuming.

"I hope to take this morning to break fast with you, as a symbol of the new day that has broken over the Cyfandir. Let us eat, enjoy, and exchange our ideas of what is to come!" He sat down while the group applauded.

A band played in the corner, light, celebratory tunes that countered a very different feel amongst the people eating. Most discussed acts of heroism from the night before, and general questions about how such a treasonous (and nearly successful) act could be planned in secret.

"I think you handled the challenge well, lad," said Artemus. "One can learn a lot about a leader when their leadership is challenged. You kept your head and took the time you needed to meet the challenge. Admirably executed."

"I agree with that sentiment," said Indaria. "Unfortunately your hand was forced, and blood was spilt, but your nation remains sound."

"I wish my Da was here." King Thannon looked the most lost. "He would have seen this coming."

"Not only that," added Alene. "He would have known how to address it. Possibly before it unfolded."

"To Bedwyn Foresight," Johan said with a raised glass, "For seeing and dealing with so many threats for so long. He is already missed."

The company repeated his toast and drank respectfully.

"Do you anticipate," asked Patrick, "any more threats, Johan?"

"An excellent question, sir," the Ivon Nova replied. "In my estimation, Vincent was never a threat. Not compared to Uvrede the Deposed. We were attacked by a great dragon of legend! Seventeen thousand years old! If it weren't for Angus activating that magical spear and sacrificing himself in an insane attack, she would still be here, terrorizing the Cyfandir.

"Things like Uvrede are the threats I am concerned with. Hundreds of years since we've seen a dragon, and we've had two attack the Cyfandir this year alone! I have reason to believe there are more. Possibly many more."

"Where are they coming from?" asked Thannon.

"The Winding." Johan pointed south.

"South of the Winding?" said Patrick with surprise. "Nothing can survive there."

"I didn't say south of the Winding. I think they live in it. On an island that is sheltered from the storms."

"That sounds like a fictional story. We've been killing the last of the dragons for generations." Artemus was convicted. "I won my kingdom from one of the last nests, a thousand years ago. These seem like stragglers to me."

"I thought the same," nodded Johan. "Until I found evidence that an orc looked up the stories of Uvrede the Deposed and Shurakhame, the Bloodhome, right before Uvrede arrived. And my account is not the only one that included an orc riding Uvrede."

"Zonka." Indaria voiced the name without thinking.

"What did you say?" demanded Ynghild.

"I said Zonka. Black Zonka." Indaria quickly considered what to share. "Zonka is an orc shaman who lives at the southern edge of our forest. She has an unnaturally long life for an orc. She is older than me, by a lot. Older than you, Artemus, and possibly even Drailin."

"Do you think it was her on the dragon?" asked Johan.

"I do. But that is all I will say for now."

"How can you know that?" asked Thannon.

"I have said all I can." Indaria rose to leave.

"Please stay, Indaria. We will not press you further." Johan punctuated his statement with stern looks at the kings across from him. Thannon pursed his lips and looked down, and Artemus raised an acquiescing hand. Indaria sat back down, a worried expression on her face, and Johan continued.

"Whomever it was, that person found something we had right here and used the knowledge against us. We can't be willfully ignorant again. I have hundreds of scholars, teachers, and bards working hard, scouring our shelves to determine what we should know. I ask that you do the same, and share any information you can with us."

"Have you learned anything else that we should act on?" asked Thannon.

"So much." Johan was emphatic. "Most of all, how much more we need to learn and relearn. The world is a much bigger place than the Cyfandir. There are other peoples. Other cultures. Each has different strengths and weaknesses.

"I don't have reason to fear any of this, except for the uncertainty of thousands of years since our last contact. I think it is time to rediscover, both the full extent of the Cyfandir and the full extent of our world."

"Do you know," Artemus asked, "what might be closest to us? Who might live there?"

"That has not been easy to decipher. I think that Mirekka may be the closest large land mass. It seems to be to the southwest, in the vicinity of the Winding. Who lives there? I can't say now. But there were humans, dwarves, elves and goblins. At one time, even orcs."

"Elves?" Indaria perked up at the thought. "You called this land Mirekka? Was it known by other names?"

"Possibly. But I mostly have Ivonian records, and they are prone to prioritize the human point of view."

"What is it like?" asked Drailin. "What is there to trade?"

"Some rumors, Drailin, suggest there may be gormoital there, among other things."

"Oh, come now, Johan," teased Ynghild. "You haven't told them the exciting part."

"Gormoital is exciting," interjected Artemus.

"Well, I'm not sure if it is true anymore."

"True or not, youngster," Artemus said, "I'll hear the exciting part. If there is something more exciting than gormoital, let's hear it!"

"Artemus, what do the Argentine Holt and Ivonia have in common?"

"They've both got a serious case of the dwarves!" joked Indaria.

"True, but not what I'm going for."

"Recently?" Artemus thought, then answered. "We've both had dragons come to visit. Are dragons attacking Mirekka?"

"You are so close!" Johan rose to stand over the rest of the people, who were still seated. "The Mirekkans, the human society there, kept dragons – and flew on them!"

The company took a full minute to process that assertion before launching into a barrage of questions.

"How is that possible," Patrick asked, "if dragons are dumb, murderous animals?"

"I'm led to believe," stated Angus, "that there is a lot more going on upstairs with dragons than many of us thought."

"That's right, Angus," said Artemus. "It took us months to sneak into the dragon's lair that is now the Argentine Holt. Thykskaal was far too cunning to be taken in a fair fight. They are definitely intelligent."

"Agreed," said Johan, "and not just because of the intelligent strategies we saw Uvrede employ here in Ivonal. From what I've read, she was the wise and respected ruler of a place they called Shurakhame. Thousands of dragons called that place home."

"This is from your Bard Corps' research?" asked Thannon.

"Some, but most of what I learned about Uvrede was what the orc – Zonka? – had researched first."

"Imagine learning something from an orc!" Angus laughed.

"You might be surprised, son," said Floin. "Artemus and I were privileged to meet some of the tribes that live in between the Argentine and Aureate. They were a peaceful group, much more than I would have expected."

"It's true," added Artemus, "so much so that some stay at the Aureate Holt now."

"Do you mean to tell me," spat Angus, "that after I faced thousands of orcs to keep them away, we're letting them in now?"

"We need the people," answered Drailin. "Even with the goblins from Seljuk, we can't keep up with the need to move materials and rebuild. So when Artemus introduced us, we had to invite them in."

Angus sat back in his chair with a defeated look. Floin patted him on the back in a paternal way.

"I never saw that coming," Angus said.

"You didn't see Szicthys coming either, now did you? Or Uvrede?" Thannon said. "Of course, neither did my da, Bedwyn."

"I wonder," said Artemus, "what Bedwyn would make of this Mirekkan talk?"

"He'd heard a bit before he passed," responded Thannon, "and he was intrigued. But dwarves aren't sailors, as a rule. He mostly wanted to know more about everyone he hadn't encountered."

"Exactly!" shouted Johan. "We need to know more. We need your people to add their stories, and the stories they know, to the library."

"Yes, Johan," Angus stated, "we've heard. And we'll grab those stories for certain."

"I'll look into it," Indaria offered. "But we need to come and learn from your library here, too."

"Please do. We'll get you anything you need."

Chapter 59

A Walk in the Park

Johan's guards stayed at the gate while he and Alene entered the famous cliff-top park that looked over the rest of the city from the southwest. It was flat and verdant, with fruit trees and other selections from around the Cyfandir. They followed the trails along the edge in a clockwise fashion. The city spread below them as they walked.

"I've missed you." Johan was simply Johan here, no affectations or signs of power.

"As have I missed you." Alene looked up into his eyes.

"You don't have to go home."

"Don't say that. I have a city to run. A people to care for."

"I'd rather you care for me. I'd be grateful to care for you - and you only - for the rest of my days."

"We don't always get what we'd rather."

"We could."

"Too many people depend on me. Too many people depend on you. We are both rebuilding our societies after war. It isn't the right time."

"It seems like it is never the right time, Alene."

"I know. But it still isn't."

"Look into your crystal ball. Tell me when you think it might be time. What needs to happen first?"

"A few seasons of peace? Time enough for us to set up the systems that will protect our peoples?"

"They can set up their own systems."

"Like the Trade Temple? No thanks! Speaking of the Trade Temple, did Melisende arrive? Tell me he isn't causing you problems."

"He did arrive. And he did make a mess on his first day here, but he's been no problem since."

"Good. You weren't running things when I sent him, but I figured it would be good to check."

"I think plenty of trouble has been sent back and forth recently. You are doing a much better job than the Regent."

"Ivonia's not looking so bad, either. Three months in, and the reports I get are positive."

They walked along the cliff edge to the south and came upon a bench at the southwestern point with a fantastic vantage for the sunset. They sat in silence for a while before Alene broke in.

"Talk to me in the spring. Let's see what transpires."

"I'll be on my way back with news of Mirekka by then. We'll have plenty to talk about."

"You really are leaving?"

"I am."

"Why, though? You have enough to worry about here."

"I have to know. I think we have an opportunity to make a better world."

"Well, you must come back. I insist."

"Of course I'll be back! I'm not abdicating the throne, just appointing Ynghild regent for a time."

"Ynghild?"

"Of course."

"Is there something going on between you two?"

"No." He paused, as her eyes burrowed tunnels into his. "Not for a long time."

"Good. Keep it that way."

"Says the woman who won't commit to a relationship."

"Can't commit. Publicly. There is a difference."

"Right. Makes perfect sense. Everything always makes sense with you."

"You know you like it.

"I do."

They watched the sun set in silence, hand in hand.

Chapter 60

A Trailing Wind

Alene snuck a single kiss as Johan saw her and her retinue off. They parted wordlessly, and again Johan was still visible on the docks as long as the harbor was in sight. Beatrice stayed below, still painting her dolls at a breakneck pace. She'd spent much of the last week here, while events unfolded on shore.

At some point, she'd made it ashore long enough to obtain more paintable doll blanks, and sent a number away to friends far and wide. Alene checked in on her, and left chuckling. It had been years since Alene had observed Beatrice in such a mood.

The wind was kind to them, pushing the yacht along with enough force to create a frothy white bow wave. Alene took her favorite position in the net just below the figurehead, bringing a book and a snack. For a while she delighted in being surrounded by dolphins surfing and jumping on either side.

Lunchtime found her and her friends leaning back against the railing with different sliced foods nestled in the dark green lettuce that Alene favored over breads. This allowed for the illusion that they all shared the same meal, but the chef had stuffed each offering with ingredients that the individuals would find pleasing. Dwarves had more meat and cheese, Alene fresh fruits and vegetables with nuts and seeds inside, and Beatrice a pumpkin mash with floppy bacon.

Thannon raised a glass to his absent father, Bedwyn. "He'd enjoy this. How can we go forward without knowing what will happen like he did?"

"That," answered Alene, "has been on my mind lately. Bedwyn always had a head start on future events. I don't know anyone else with that talent. I don't suppose it might run in the family?"

"If it does," said Thannon, "I'm not aware of it."

"Perhaps," interjected Beatrice, "you should look to other sources of wisdom for a while. I know a dozen women I'd trust to help you understand what is going on, Alene. Say the word, and they'll come running."

"Thank you, Bea. But I'm afraid I have to do this on my own." She considered something for a moment, and added, "However, I'd love to have a group of people with their ears to the ground, if you think any would be interested…"

"We'll talk." Beatrice smiled into her cup.

Alene changed the subject.

"How are your people dealing with the change in leadership?" she asked Thannon.

"That, my dear, is an interesting question, with an interesting answer. Da set up so many systems that, in many ways, the holt runs itself. But in others, it is clear that he took all of the responsibility. Functionally, there has been very little issue. I've met with all of the leaders in various areas and established my trust for their judgement.

"But regarding defenses and world events, and how the Holt should interact with them? Each of those demands my full attention, and I don't have as ready of an answer as Bedwyn would have. He was, quite literally, better than I."

"I feel that sentiment, Thannon," responded Alene, leaning on a taut line. "I have no memory of my mother, but everything Bea taught me, and every bit of evidence I find at the Veyns, says that I will never be able to measure up."

Bea smacked the railing to emphasize her answer.

"Nonsense! You are every bit the great woman your mother was. You have done an exceptional job of taking the Veyns back and setting up a better life for your people. I loved your mother, but I love you no less. Perhaps a lot more."

"I love you, too, Bea," Alene smiled. "And you taught me well. I can't imagine a more appropriate education for my role now than what you provided me."

Beatrice's face flickered momentarily with a very different emotion, then returned to her constant matronly glee. "I certainly tried, dear. I did my best."

Thannon changed the subject.

"How is your new trade system working out, Alene?"

"Surprisingly well, thanks. My warehouses are overflowing, but the math is mathing. We've had enough turnover in stock that my initial investment has already been recouped, and the churn should be self-sustaining for a while. I've been very lucky."

"Thannon," asked Drailin, "what do you think Bedwyn would have suggested for our next steps?"

"He'd want information first. Da was never one to make an uninformed decision. I, for instance, have no idea what lies beyond Ivonia and the Veyns. Where is this Mirekka? Are there people still living there? Are they a threat?"

"I'll go." Alene's voice was loud and sudden. "The Veyns have a long-standing tradition of seafaring and exploration. I will start with a Cartographic transit all the way around the Cyfandir, then we'll see where we go from there."

"You go to trade from there. Make agreements that encourage people to come to the Veyns with their wares, or at least to welcome and trade with Veynsian-flagged ships." Beatrice spoke calmly, with a matter-of-fact attitude.

"You should have been Queen, Bea. You were always better at it than me," said Alene.

Beatrice chuckled and rose to leave.

"I've got a doll to paint. Thannon, when I'm done, would you please deliver it to a friend, Grimal, a resident of your holt?

"Anything for you, young lady."

"Young lady, he says," she guffawed. "That was a long time ago!"

Alene watched her mentor go below decks, then continued.

"Don't let her fool you. That woman is a force of nature."

"You'd have to fool me to say otherwise!" laughed Drailin. "There is more than meets the eye in that one."

Chapter 61

Homewood Bound

"Are you sure you won't take my carriage? It is the smoothest ride you've ever enjoyed!" The Ivon Nova offered again.

"No thank you, Johan," replied Indaria. "I prefer to travel with no pomp and little circumstance."

"At least let me send a contingent to keep you safe."

"We'll be fine," she smiled, looking at her travelling companion. "I've got the greatest hero on the Cyfandir with me."

"I wouldn't say that," replied Angus. "I've been lucky."

"Perhaps," she said. "But tell me how many heroes have killed not one, but two dragons? Once might be lucky. Twice? Nobody is that lucky, Angus."

"She's right, Angus," Johan said. "We've both seen you under pressure. You are much more than lucky. And we are lucky to count you among our friends."

----- -----

Hours down the road, they rolled through the Greenway. The town was vibrant, filled with smiling faces. They broke for lunch, and continued on to the Sliver. Angus noticed the faster pace the horse that hauled their wagon made, twice the speed that he was used to. The wood of the wagon was supple and absorbed the bumps, too. The dwarf asked about it several miles north of town.

"This speed should be exhausting our animal and destroying the wagon, but I barely feel the ruts and potholes. Is that you?"

"I'll admit to it, yes. You know how the Dreamvine changed you? It changed me, too. I am significantly more powerful than I was, and I can encourage horses to move more efficiently, and even the dead boards of a wagon to be compliant. It might be seen as an abuse of power, but you've earned an easy journey for once."

"I'll take it. But I don't understand how your power grew just from being inside a vine."

"The Dreamvine is so much more than a simple plant, Angus. While inside, I became comfortable with thinking in the terms that are required. The communication I used to have to work for just comes naturally now. As long as I am there, the elven forest is safe."

"And while you aren't there?"

She laughed.

"My father, whom you have met, is not without power. In some ways, his exceeds mine – for now. Any invader would be wise to choose a different target."

"What about the times he leaves?"

"I can't remember such a time. The circumstances that would be required to have him risk leaving have not occurred in my lifetime."

"It can't be that rare. You've left twice in the short time I've known you."

"That is true."

"Is it less risky for you to leave?"

"If you ask Endaria, it is a bigger risk for me to leave."

"And yet he lets you."

Indaria didn't answer that.

----- -----

They left the Sliver without incident, and made the southern border of the forest by noon. Almost as soon as they crossed into the shade of the first tree, a thin tendril of forest vine shot out and wrapped around Angus' neck, lifting him high into the canopy and further into the forest proper. Wind whooshed past Angus' ears as he was choked and dragged what seemed like miles in mere moments.

Then he was face to face with Endaria lo Thenalah, Speaker for the woodland elves, two hundred feet off the ground. More vines wrapped around and through Angus' legs, threatening his unarmored bits, but taking some weight off of his neck and allowing his blue-tinged cheeks to regain his ruddy color.

"Where did you take my daughter?" yelled the elder elf.

"I'm sorry?" Angus coughed.

"She was here, then she was gone, and I believe you were at fault."

"I didn't–" Angus started, but the vine choked his breath away again.

"My daughter is the most important thing in the world to me. She disappeared, and you accompany her upon her return. That leads me to believe you were involved in her disappearance. I'm tempted to allow this vine to finish its job and use you for fertilizer."

"Father, he had nothing to do with my trip. He's only helped me return." Indaria floated on a different vine, several feet away and down from her father. "I was never in any danger."

Endaria looked past the captive dwarf's eyes, peering deeply into his skull. "Interesting. You did not steal her. But she was in combat. She slew six– sixty-two? You allowed my daughter to enter combat?" The vines tensed around Angus' neck again.

"No, father!" Indaria was shouting now. "I *chose* to follow the dwarves to Ivonal. I *chose* to put myself into the Garden. And I *chose* to save several dwarves from combat by capturing and dealing with the men who pursued them and the Ivon Nova."

"The Garden?"

Angus gasped, trying to breathe. Endaria let the vine loosen its chokehold.

"Oh. I'm sorry, I was being rash. Daughter, tell me about the Garden. I thought it was gone."

"Far from it. The elves who tended it have been gone a long time, but Ivonians try from time to time. Usually butchering good plants while they are at it. It is time for a new Shepherd."

"As I feared, I have not heard from the last one in generations."

"She lives."

Angus was dropped by the vine as Endaria's attention lapsed. After a second of freefall he howled in terror, finding himself caught by several vines from two directions. These slowly lowered him to the ground.

"Did you commune with her?"

"I did, but only enough to consider the next step. We can talk about what that entails later, when we don't have a dwarf in earshot."

The dwarf, as it happened, was not in earshot. He was picking up his gear and headed for his wagon, trying to make his escape while he could. Indaria directed the plants to lower her to the ground near Angus.

"You won't get away that easily, my young friend." She moved toward him for a farewell embrace. He didn't resist. "Travel safely, and come back to visit."

"Come here?" He replied incredulously. "For a visit? A social visit? You must be mad!" He smiled to reveal his jibe. "But of course, as long as your father doesn't try to kill me again."

Endaria's feet alighted on a bed of soft moss, which did not indent under his weight. "My dear dwarf, if I had tried to kill you, you'd know it. It would be the last thing you knew. As uncomfortable as you've found my forest, we've given you and yours more latitude than anyone else in hundreds of years. I actually hold you in high regard!"

"High regard? You were holding me high, but by the throat!"

"I apologize for my rudeness. I was concerned for my daughter and my family's safety. I wanted to get your attention."

"You have it, Speaker."

"Father." Indaria said with a stern look.

"Yes, all right. Angus, I will not assault you in the future unless you are an immediate threat."

"Thank you. I'll not be a threat to you or your family, Speaker. Your daughter has become as close as family to me recently. I would never harm her."

Chapter 62

Fait Accompli

Angus found his way cleared and straight, with no further interference from Indaria or her father. He rode into the night to reach the Holt without stopping. He paid a youngster dwarfing the stables to unload his gear for him, made his way to the new place in the Upper Diggins, and crashed onto his bed.

He awoke to sounds of sizzling and humming from the kitchen he shared with his father. He rose and freshened up, then joined Floin at the table.

"Good lighting[15], Da."

"Good lighting, boy! How did you rest?"

"I slept deeply. It is so good to be home."

"Aye. We've missed you. And now you can stay a while, I hope? There are a lot of dwarves that would like to catch up with you. They want to hear all about your journeys."

"I don't know what they'd be interested in that hasn't been told already."

Floin slid a plate across the ornate oak table to Angus. It was overloaded with the best sausages and eggs laden with exotic cheeses, and some spilled as it schlid to a stop in front of him. Silverware, well-worked solid silverware, arrived next.

"Angus. Remember over the winter, when you and I had to buy the older bread and hunks of cheese with mold we'd need to trim? Do you remember when we'd have to brew tea more than once with the same leaves? Look at us now.

"We eat like kings. Like literal kings! And you are friends with kings! Artemus invites me on vacations. You are on a first name

15 Dwarves in the Holt don't depend strictly on the sun like surface dweller's do; so they mark times of day with the quality of light. 'Good lighting' would translate roughly to 'good morning,' but it might occur at any point compared to the outside. In this case, either would be somewhat accurate, as it actually was mid-morning at the surface.

basis with the leaders of every holt, group, and nation! Who is to blame for that?

"A single accident, I know."

"Nonsense! Your first kill might have been an accident, but given another half-second, might you have made the same decision?"

"I don't think so, but it is possible."

"Right! It is possible! So, your entire journey towards heroism and fame started with an accidental move that you might have performed in another moment intentionally. It counts as a heroic action, whether you intended it or not!"

"That's not what Artemus said."

Someone knocked at the door, and Floin jumped up to answer. As if bidden, Mountain King Artemus entered.

"Thanks for the breakfast[16] invite, Floin. I've already eaten, but I've never turned down a second breakfast!" He patted his paunch meaningfully.

"Of course! Have a seat, I'll bring a small serving over."

Floin followed this up with a plate piled six inches high, carefully laid right in front of the King, who attacked it with a smile.

"We were just talking about you," Angus said. "I was trying to convince Da that you don't approve of how I killed Szicthys. Would you tell him?"

"Oh, I didn't approve," said the King past the sausage he was chewing. "But I do now. That one little moment is something that's weighed heavily on me for months. But I've come to accept that you were in a position to make the same decision as soon as it occurred to you."

"But," responded Angus, "what if it never occurred to me?"

"Aye," said the King, "that was heavily on my mind. Before that moment, you hadn't been in those situations. We'd never seen what you could or would do when the time came. But in these last six months, you've shown your quality time and time again.

"You've shown us that you would –and do– make those split-second decisions. That you see what to do and do it without

16 Dwarves may not use morning for the aforementioned reasons, but breakfast is still used as they are literally breaking the fast.

hesitation. Over and over and over again. So, while you've admitted that the first kill was accidental, I'm convinced you'd have done it either way."

Angus looked at the two elder dwarves, then down at his food. Before that moment, he'd have insisted he'd never make a leap like that, but Artemus had a point.

"It kind of strains the mind to think of it. Like an animal shipped in a crate. When it arrives, is it alive or dead? And does the act of opening the crate save it, or kill it? I see your point, anyway. Or do I?"

"Angus, I gave you six months to prove that you were a hero. I sent you on a mission that might have put you in situations to be tried –maybe you'd get an opportunity or two. But now that you are back, I don't think you are a hero."

"See, Da? Not a hero." Angus jerked a thumb at himself.

"Not a hero," Artemus continued. "Angus Dragonbane, you are a craggy legend!"

Chapter 63

Ivon Mirekka

"I'm going to miss this." The Ivon Nova said from his luxurious bath as his Second shaved him.

"I don't understand," responded Ynghild.

"Being pampered. Not having to lift a finger if I don't want to. You've made being Ivon an easy, confident experience."

"I exist to serve."

"That's not true and you know it. But you are very good at making men think they are the most important person in the world."

"...says the most powerful man on the Cyfandir. In your case, it is true."

"What if it wasn't true?"

She finished the last stroke, rinsed the razor, and carried it back to its case while drying it with a towel.

"But it is. You've made the Cyfandir a safer place. You've brought people together. I'd argue, Johan, that you are the most important person in the world. At least on the Cyfandir."

"It wasn't just me. Several others, yourself included, played a big role and hundreds more made a difference."

"Who made the plan?"

"Touché."

"Now that we've established that," she continued, "why would it possibly change?"

"You said it yourself. The Cyfandir is safe. Mirekka beckons."

"So, send an expedition. Learn what you must to get the peace you deserve."

"That's not the way I work, Yng. I have to go myself."

"You can't leave now. We've just started a time of stability."

"Exactly. Stability. People know who governs Ivonia, and how."

"If you leave, there would be chaos."

"Who runs Ivonia, Yng?"

"You, of course."

"I make final decisions, certainly. But who does all of the actual work? Who makes the connections, grants commissions, and issues directives?"

Ynghild did not answer. After a moment, Johan continued.

"You do, Ynghild. Not the Angel, but the Second. And now it is time for you to advance."

"I don't want to be the Ivon."

"Of course you don't."

"What then?"

"Stay here and be the Regent. Ivonia's first in two hundred years. Continue to run the city as you have been."

"For how long?"

"As long as it takes."

"No."

"No?"

"You heard me. No."

"Why not, Yng?"

"I will not be trapped in a limited position forever. We saw what that did to the Veyns."

"I follow you. So, what are your terms?"

"I'll give you two years as regent. If you come back in that time, you keep going as the Ivon. If you are gone for two years, then I become the Ivon with all that entails."

He studied her. It was a fair ask. And if he took longer than two years, he was probably dead, a real possibility in the Winding. If he passed, any other process would likely lead to bloodshed.

"Done. Draw up the edict, and I'll sign it. I'd like to outfit the *Hidden Queen* for the expedition. Please see if she's in port."

Ynghild started towards the stairway and paused.

"Are you sure this is what you want?"

"Not at all. But I think it is what needs to happen. You were born for this. And I…" he looked out the window, past the harbor,

"I need to know. I need to know what lies at Mirekka. Are the people still there? The dwarves? The dragons?"

"The Ivon Nova is still a bard." She sighed. "Go then. And come back to me. This can't be the end of our story."

"I intend to return," he said. *But not to you*, he thought. "This is not the end of the story. As the Cyfandric Cycle –that's what I'm calling it– wraps up for a time, the Mirekkan Cycle begins. And what a story that will be!"

A note from the author:

Thank you so much for coming with me on this journey through the Harkentale Saga!

These first four books, a quartet, represent the Cyfandric Cycle, a period of awakening and disruption on the land mass the locals call "the Cyfandir."

Holtgart
Pickled Marble
Dreamvine
Ivon Nova

These events have led to the rediscovery of a long-forgotten island nation called Mirekka. Driven by his passion for learning the true stories of the larger world, Johan C'Antrell, Ivon Nova, leads an expedition of rediscovery to learn the secrets of Mirekka in the next quartet of the Harkentale Saga, the Mirekkan Cycle. I hope you'll come along as these are planned for release in 2026!

Bard Corps
Feldwood
Wyrmhaule
Khartlore

-Jeremy James Smith

Enjoying the Harkentale Saga?

Find more information
and merchandise

at

Harkentale.com

To keep up with releases and events,
subscribe to the
Harkentale newsletter
and follow on social media

@Harkentale

Made in the USA
Columbia, SC
08 July 2025

60408076R00136